MARKS
OF A
CHANGING
SITUATION

Jake Hampson

ISBN 978-1-957220-87-1 (paperback)
ISBN 978-1-957220-88-8 (hardcover)
ISBN 978-1-957220-89-5 (digital)

Rushmore Press LLC
1 800 460 9188
www.rushmorepress.com

Printed in the United States of America

All italics in the book between characters communicating is in sign language. This will mostly be done, as shown below. Italics will also be used to show emphasis mostly in one word uses.

Hello, my name is Mark. How are you doing? Signed Mark.

Contents

Chapter One

SHIFTING HOME

MY LIFE WAS SHIFTING and changing; I'm not sure if it was for the better or worse. My brother gave me an offer at the art sale to come and live with him. I would never have expected this, an offer to move in and live with him. I can finally escape my parents and hopefully have a better life with my brother. I wanted to live a life where I didn't need to mask and hide away. I could hopefully do my stimming freely soon. I wanted to do various sensory interactions, such as laying with my weighted blanket or using chewies. That life was almost in my grasp, but only if Josh held true to his words. Until then, I would need to be careful with what might happen. My love for my brother constantly changed ever since he left for college. I didn't know what to think when he came back a changed person, only to revert to who he had been before he left for college that first time. I wanted him to remain the brother I grew to care for and love. I hoped that would be the person he showed me now that we would live together.

For a few moments, I contemplated my reaction to what my brother said about me moving in with him. I wanted it to be true: a new reality and home. Josh said, "I want you to leave our parents. I learned what's happened since I left. I am sorry." I'm not sure what Josh meant by being sorry, as if it was his fault, but I wanted to believe that his offer was real.

I stood up from the floor where I sat after accepting Josh's offer to go and live with him instead of our parents. My feet moved forward, taking me to my tables. The sale closed, but I hadn't packed yet. I carefully placed all the artwork into duffle bags so they could go back with me to Josh's apartment. Luckily, the bags filled up quickly.

Moving the bags around, I saw Dr. Joe standing nearby with a smile on his face. I nodded back. Josh had asked earlier if he could help me load up his car with items so we could go straight back to his apartment tonight and continue packing tomorrow. I followed the large multi-colored duffle bag out of the building and a small car with a good-sized trunk. We started to load all the bags into the trunk and back seat. I didn't pay attention to how the car looked, my mind swirling with too many thoughts.

I still felt confused by the fact that Josh invited me to live with him so close to the end of his summer break. He seemed the closest to having the same beliefs as my parents. Though I couldn't remember him ever trying to change how I acted, Josh would just make insinuations about what was happening in my school, just like they would do.

Never had I been as happy as when Josh returned from college. He seemed like a new person due to the influences of new people around him; the cycle for the past four years of Josh leaving and coming back before changing again every year. To me, his changes felt like the tide or the moon, subtle but noticeable. Still, I needed to figure out what to do and how to act now that I moved in with a person who recently thought I couldn't function. Until I proved him wrong, and he had a long talk with Dr. Joe, one of my friends' dads.

The car lurched forward after we had finished packing, and Josh asked me if I wanted to listen to some music. I shrugged at that question, not sure how to answer it. Normally, I would just listen to others played in the car, as I only listened to music around others or tried to block out the world.

The drive back to where Josh lived was quiet until Josh broke the silence and said, "Mark, Dr. Joe told me you normally go out to eat with your friends after one of your sales. If you want, I can take you somewhere to eat before we get to my apartment?" Josh's voice sounded weird in my head, as I hadn't really heard him talk like that around me. He asked me what I wanted instead of assuming based on what I liked when I was younger.

Out of my mouth, I said, "Sure. That works." My voice sounded dull instead of the normal upbeat tone I had when I would normally be asked where I wanted to go. Now I just felt numb to the world, not knowing what to think. I wanted to find a new home and place to live, but I never thought it would be with my brother.

In an upbeat tone, Josh said back to me, "Okay, what do you want to get? We should probably get the food to go so we can get you home as it has been a long day." There it was, that tone that I hadn't heard out of Josh before. I didn't know what the tone meant in terms of Josh, but normally, I believe it showed caring.

Where Josh planned on taking me, I was unsure, but I would enjoy the ride to where we headed. I couldn't decide on what I wanted, so I didn't really care where we went. I told Josh that I didn't care what we would be getting if it was filling, as I had forgotten to eat lunch.

We pulled over to a restaurant, and Josh got us some burgers and a container of ice cream for us to share. I quietly ate my burger as we drove down the road to where I hoped I would soon call home. After eating, I began to doze off and fell asleep in the moving car.

The day after the art fair where Josh asked me to move in with him, Josh would be taking me back to my parents' house to grab the basics and some art supplies. I was happy to be leaving. I was getting out of my parents' grip and into the looser one of my brothers'. My phone buzzed, and I pulled it out to look at the screen; it was a text from Steve. He sadly didn't manage to make it to my art sale when I invited him after helping me with being overwhelmed by the school's outside area. I wish that he had been able to make it, but he didn't show up. I hope we didn't miss each other at the sale. I got a text from Steve saying that he couldn't find a ride to the art sale yesterday. I'm glad that Steve didn't forget. Maybe next time, I should ask if I can offer him a ride to come to the art sale. I texted back asking if he wanted to know what I had to sell, and he texted back quickly with a yes.

That brought a smile to my face, another person interested in my art without even seeing it! I was getting excited. The way my parents talked to me about my dream of being an artist still affects me. Even though I got many commissions and sales, I am still nervous about my choice. I remember my parent's words. "You will never be able to make a living by relying upon others to buy your crafts." This is ironic, as my parents make furniture. Steve started to text, looking back at the phone, and there was a half-made message. I finished my message and hit send asking if there is anything specific he wanted.

I was unsure and nervous, as I had sold to my friends and random people before, but not people who helped me with sensory overload. I could tell that Steve was a safe person, but I wasn't sure if I would scare him off for what he helped me through. I didn't want to risk losing a potential friend over him not liking my art or a disagreement about the price or style. I wanted to keep Steve as a potential friend and didn't want to risk losing him before getting to possibly being friends with him. I replied with all the art and craft projects I made and still had left. There were many of the projects I made still in my possession that I didn't manage to sell in the sale, though I did sell most of the weavings I made. I didn't know Steve that well so I was curious about how he would respond. A person can learn a lot based on the art they buy. Steve replied by asking for a drawing though he didn't say what type he wanted.

I told him what I didn't sell, but I didn't know what Steve would want. I wasn't sure if I would have what he wanted and didn't want to disappoint. After a few moments, Steve asked if I had any animal drawings. Sadly, I sold all the premade ready-to-sell ones of that style drawing, so I asked if he was okay with waiting or possibly doing a commission. I hope Steve is okay with that as it will be more expensive. I'm capable of many different art styles, so I hope I can make something he likes. It all depends on what I am asked to make.

A few minutes passed, and he replied, asking how much a commission would be. After replying that it would depend on what he wanted and the size, I sat and waited for a reply. Steve then texted back, asking if I was able to do a deer in a clearing and that he would send me a reference image. I looked at the image and was able to think of a simple sketch to start with though how complex the final image would depend on other factors. Does he want it in color or black and white? How detailed should it be? After hammering out the color, which would be in black and white, and the amount of detail that Steve wanted in the drawing, we planned out a meeting for the next day around 8 AM. I was nervous but happy about what would happen tomorrow.

From the apartment hallway, I heard Josh say, "Hey, Mark, it's time to go and pack up some of your room," one of the parts I had been dreading. I had been chewing my lip for the whole day and almost forgot that I needed to pack up my old room with the excitement over moving out and texting with Steve. I didn't want to return home, and I didn't know how to share that with Josh.

Standing up, I grabbed my clothes and got dressed. I put on some soft socks designed for hiking that Josh gave me as a gift when we'd reached his apartment, a pair of shorts that were loose but had a tighter thermal layer underneath. They were a nice dark blue with an electric blue line to outline the darker sides. They provided a nice sensation and helped me to be able to focus on the texture when I walked and not get too cold. After the shorts, I put on the socks Josh gave me. After that, I put on a textured t-shirt with a t-dye design that I had done myself. The shirt's design swirled out from the center and moved in a pattern like a whirlpool going from the center out in a mixture of dark and light blues. Josh had been nice, even giving me a set of noise-canceling sensory headphones.

Josh told me he'd bought them as a present to be given at the end of school and forgot to give them to me. Josh's original plan was for me to move in with him after he rented the apartment so I would leave our parents' house. Sadly, he forgot that plan partway through the summer and only remembered after talking with someone named George. George was someone Josh met at college who apparently was one of the people who recommended the plan.

Chapter Two
MEETING POSSIBLE HELP

GETTING OUT OF THE car, I moved to the door of my parents' house. My nervousness returned full force as I neared the front door. Josh was ahead of me. My slow-moving feet shuffled on the hard concrete. I wanted the ground to sink and pull me in so I would have a reason to avoid this. After a time that seemed to move too quickly, I reached the door with Josh. He tried to open the door, but it was locked. Reaching into his pocket, he pulled out a key and unlocked the house, and we headed inside. I joined him and moved toward my room, not wanting to make any loud noises. I didn't want to be more overwhelmed than I already was.

"So, Mark, are you ready to pack?" I jumped slightly, my body tensing at the sound, waiting for someone to appear. I think I felt how a surprised child would when facing a new situation. Josh turned to me and said, "Come on, Mark, let's head up to your room." Josh was too loud for the moment. A headache started to form, and my head began to pound. It was like I was being stabbed.

Josh and I headed up the stairs. When we reached the door to my room, Josh tried to open the door, not realizing it had two locks. I stepped forward, pulling my keys out of my pocket. I fumbled with the keys, causing a jingling sound to go around. A sharp pain hit my head, and I rushed to open the door. It unlocked, and I flung it open, causing a small slamming sound.

I rushed to my bed, grabbed my sunglasses on the nightstand, and buried my head into the blankets. I grabbed my weighted blanket and pulled it over myself as I curled up to block the sensory input. I liked the weight as it helped calm me down and let me ignore parts of the world while focusing on other areas.

I had forgotten my sunglasses. I couldn't forget my wallet and keys due to missing the sensory information if I didn't have them in my pockets.

A new weight joined me on my bed. "Hey, Mark, are you OK?" I couldn't see Josh, but his voice was a gentle, low sound.

Raising my hand, I signed *No.* Curling further into the bed, I ignored the world and tried to decrease my headache and not become overwhelmed. There was a swooshing sound, and the light decreased. A door clicked closed, and I listened, and footsteps walked over to my bed; they stopped, and a weight joined me on the end of the bed. "May I try and help? One of my friends gets sensory overload, and I am guessing that's what's happening. I can try to do what I do to help them."

I signed back; *yes*. My hand shook from the effort of such an action. I wasn't sure what he would do, but I hoped it would help. If it didn't, I had the option to move away. I would like to learn other ways that might help me to be less overwhelmed.

Josh lifted the blankets a little to put a small thing of soft fabric in my open hand. "Alright, Mark, squeeze this; it might help." I squeezed the pile of fabric and just waited. He told me to try and think of happy moments.

Out of my pile of blankets, I peeked my head out, and Josh smiled at me. Out the window, clouds now had passed over the sun blocking the light from entering through the window. "Are you doing better now?" I nodded my head and got up, ready to help a bit but still unable to talk for the moment. "Alright then. Do you think you are ready to start packing?"

I signed *yes* instead of speaking as I didn't want to talk.

I moved over to my closet and pulled out a few of my old backpacks. I started to stack books and stuff them into the bags. Josh moved over, grabbed a couple of yarn bundles, and put them into a nearby empty garbage bag. He explained that this was to store delicate items, as it was easier to move them in that style of bag. We planned to write labels directly on the bags.

I continued grabbing books and binders of old artwork from school that I hadn't sold or that were originals I kept using as reference material. I carefully put them into my padded, water-resistant bags.

I continued packing, grabbing an old box of papers I had written back at the start of middle school. The box burst open and fell out all over the floor. There was a crumpled envelope with my parent's name written on it. I never did give them this letter as I was too scared of what might happen. I guess I might as well attempt to read the letter again after all these years to see if I felt the same way now as I did back then. I opened the envelope and started to read. My head ached. My handwriting was poor back then, and my hands had been shaky while I was writing the letter. I was glad my teacher never read it and had just told us to give it to the person if we were comfortable.

Chapter Three
READING FORGOTTEN WORDS

As the paper unfolded, the old letter was in my barely legible handwriting. I had trouble reading and needed to pause as I tried to decipher my handwriting. I remembered what I wrote even after all these years due to the amount of effort I had put into making it look legible. As I read, I noticed how my writing has improved over the years since I first wrote the words.

Dear Mom and Dad,

I don't know how to help you to know my pain. I know you don't see how I feel. You don't accept who I am because you can't see me, and you don't see how I want to change. I want you to see who I am, but I feel the need to hide what you tell me. Living in pain, little go through and those who don't, don't understand. I don't know what to do to help with the pain that you always see me in.

I never know when I'll get overloaded. I don't know how to let others who don't know how to help me and who don't accept me. I can sometimes predict the cause, but often, it will happen without notice. I know you don't think my pain is real, but it is. I live with parts of life that you don't understand, but I want you to know what happens. This is who I am. I need help sometimes, or else, I will break down and not be able to function. Please accept that this is who I am in terms of my autism.

I have ADHD, which means I can't focus sometimes, and I get distracted. Please see me. I don't focus well, and I get distracted, but I can learn a new subject sometimes. I'm working on focusing, but sometimes, I fail. Like with art, I can focus if I am interested, but I can't do it if I'm not. This is my life. I want you to accept me. Please see me as I am and not what you want me to be. I don't want to disappoint you.

Sincerely, Mark

I guess I must have paused for a bit, as Josh was standing next to me the next thing I knew. "Are you doing OK, Mark?"

"Yes, I'm fine, Josh. Just found an old letter." I didn't recognize my emotions were all over the place, but I didn't know how to tell Josh that.

"Who is it to, or from, if you are willing to share?" I didn't say a thing; I just continued to pack as I shoved the letter into a bag going with me in the front seat of the car. The bag was an old backpack, well-loved and worn. A deep blueish green with a few embroidered areas of fraying black and blue thread covered my bag. It held my different sensory tools like chewies, weighted lap blankets, and fidgets. I used my chewies every so often. I usually used the necklaces for chewing, so I wouldn't chew on my shirts or lip. One of my favorites was a little snake-like contraption that turned and twisted around. In the bag were my phone charger and the smaller blankets I slept with.

I grabbed the bags I had packed, moving to head out, and Josh joined me. I walked to the door and hoped that our parents wouldn't make an appearance. I walked quickly to my bedroom door and into the hallway. There was a loud slam and what sounded like my parents' voices from below.

I rushed back into the room, crashed into the bed, dropped the bags on the floor, and curled up in my blankets. I wrapped my head up and vanished into the darkness my blankets provided.

While I tried to calm down my beating heart, I didn't know what to do. Blindly reaching out, I grabbed the pair of earbuds I had left on my bedside table. I put in the earbuds and sighed in relief. The light of my room was still too bright. I curled further into my blankets pile, hiding away. From near the doorway to the room, there were footsteps that were faint, and I heard the light switch turn off. The light in the room decreased, but the sun still shined strong into my blanket pile with my head buried underneath dimmed from under my blanket pile.

"Mark, is that better?" Josh said in a quiet voice. With how overwhelmed I was, he may as well have been shouting.

I raised a shaking hand; I signed *yes*.

"OK, then Mark, just calm down. Why are you curled up like that?" I didn't respond as I couldn't speak yet, and my sign wouldn't show. "OK, keep calm, Mark. Everything will be OK. I will wait with you until you are doing better and are up to leaving. If you need anything, fingerspell me what you need."

I fingerspelled, *OK*.

I hadn't had a family member near me during one of my sensory overloads since I was a young child or during the car ride where they would just think I was sleeping. I had been alone at home, experiencing this life by myself, even though many were home, all because I was alone in my room. Now I had a family member with me who was accepting and offering me comfort.

The downstairs door creaked open and our dad yelled, "Josh, are you home? Your car was in the street." Josh remained quiet, and our parents were downstairs by the stair before they headed up the stairs. Dad knocked on the door to my room and asked, "Josh, are you in there packing with Mark?" "Yes, Dad, I am." Josh's voice had a hesitation to it, but it was sturdy. The weight shifted more to my bed, next to my feet.

After that response, our dad paused before he replied, "Okay, are you two done packing for now?"

"Not yet. We are taking a break, and I can't talk now; I need to help Mark." Josh's voice got stronger and was apparently easily heard through the door, but it was still quite enough for me. I started to shake due to how loud my dad's voice was and Josh's growing volume.

Dad grew louder as he said, "Fine, then when Mark is done with his little fit, come out and say hi." The footsteps loudly headed down the stairs, stomping, causing me to wince back at the sound.

"Sorry about that. Let's just wait here. Let me know when you are ready to leave." Josh's voice was quiet and peaceful, unlike how he normally spoke to me. He normally didn't change his volume like he was doing now. My headache was lessening, and slowly, my voice began to return. I poked my head out of my blanket pile. Josh was sitting on the bed looking at me. "Are you ready to go, Mark?"

Yes. Let's go. I still didn't want to talk even though I felt like I could, but I grabbed my various bags and moved to the door. My ears were plugged with headphones, and I had a clear goal of easing my aching mind. I headed out of my bedroom door; Josh followed behind me. As we entered the hallway, I faintly heard talking from downstairs. Josh and I reached the wide staircase. My parents' words became clearer, though the voices were distorted by my headphones. I waited at the top of the stairs to listen.

I first heard my dad talk. "Honey, why does Mark throw those fits? I don't know what to do when he has them. They bring so much attention to us when we leave the house—I just don't know how to describe them. They are just so loud, or he just stops doing anything. I don't know what to do. Now it seems he has Josh to help him." His voice was loud and sounded like rumbling thunder when he talked about when I got overwhelmed by the world.

"Brent, maybe this is a good thing. Now that Mark is moving out, maybe we can adapt. Maybe we can learn to help him." Moms' voice was at a lower volume. Her voice carried through the house to me clearly like I was in the room, reverberating through my body.

"Heather, you know we can't do that. People are faking disabilities. I want to help them, but they may be faking it to make work easier. What should we do when Mark can speak, but he refuses to? I don't want to accommodate him when it is unneeded."

Why would Dad say that? I tried to teach them that Sign Language would help them with multiple people in their line of work. It helps them communicate with people who are deaf or mute. Sign language is versatile and can be impactful across rooms. I didn't realize they saw it as me trying to force them into a different way of life when all I wanted was to communicate, especially when I wasn't able to do anything else. What did my parents want me to do?

My mom waited for a bit, then started to talk. "I understand, Brent. I don't want to enable him either, but maybe we should learn to sign to help those living near us who are deaf or mute. If we do that, then we can also help Mark."

I didn't know they had these discussions. Why wouldn't they talk to me? I might have been able to try and describe why I don't speak. I would've been able to try and help them to understand. I wanted to go downstairs, but I couldn't seem to move.

My dad responded almost immediately to what my mom had said. "I understand that, Heather, but we don't have the time. Besides, Mark can speak, and he can hear, so he should communicate verbally. He also shouldn't throw those fits willy-nilly. He should at least do them in his room and not outside around others. It's embarrassing to stand out like that in the crowd. I wish that he wouldn't just collapse to the ground or not be able to move without us forcing him to, as that makes us seem like we aren't raising our kid right."

Dad claimed he was willing to accommodate, but he claimed he didn't have the time. Who should I believe my experience or new information I had never heard before? Why hadn't my parents tried to talk to me about this? I know we already had a different communication method. So why would he need to learn my preferred method when one already works in his eyes?

I wondered why they didn't use those communication methods with me instead of forcing me to talk? My parents claimed they were able to write back and forth with their deaf friends, so why not with me? My breathing was growing heavy. I couldn't see what was happening, but I liked to imagine my parents sitting together and talking, not yelling like how loud their voices seemed to me.

"Brent, remember we were told that people can't control when they get sensory overload. I think that's what it was called. I wish Mark would give us a warning, so we might be able to help him before he shut down. I want to help, but no one tells us exactly what to do because they claim everyone's situation is different every time. So, what should we do but wait and see, even if I don't know what to do?" Mom also cared and wanted to help but didn't know-how. "I still want to support Mark."

They could have asked me, but they didn't. I wasn't asked about any of this; just ignored and not accepted. My thoughts were getting louder, and my headache was returning. I wanted to sit down, but I couldn't, with all the bags I had around me.

"Heather, that doesn't matter. He should still try and warn us or give us a cue. I don't know what to do with him. How can we work with his problems when he doesn't tell us anything?" Dad's voice was steadily growing louder as he spoke. "He is just so confusing I don't know what to do. How should we handle this? He is moving out. We won't have to see his problems in our face every day now." His words pierced through my head.

Knowing my dad, he would be walking around in front of whomever he was talking to. In my head, I saw him pacing up and down the rug in the living room like he did when I did something in public he didn't like, and he would take me home to talk with me about that behavior.

"Brent, I know. I am also confused, but we can still offer to help if we just talk. We have been ignoring this for so long. Maybe we should try to change?" Mom's voice broke as she spoke. I imagined tears forming on her face. That was the voice my mom often used when she was crying.

"Stay strong, Heather. We need to be strong; we can't break. I don't understand this autism, but that doesn't mean we are in the wrong. We don't know what to do, but that isn't our fault. None of the training we could have gone to would have helped us. We are doing our best, and Josh can help Mark more than we can right now. Don't worry, honey; things will get better." Dad's voice was getting quieter and more calming as he spoke.

I stopped but couldn't move yet due to the views I'd heard. My body paused for a moment, then reverted to pre-sensory overload. I still felt overwhelmed, but I wasn't shutting down anymore, and I could kind of focus on what I wanted to do without being completely locked away.

Chapter Four
CONFRONTATION OF FAMILY

I heard enough and decided to head downstairs. My footfalls sounded heavy and loud to me. I pushed through the pain and continued my descent. As I reached the bottom stair, my parent was dressed nicely, and I guessed they had gone somewhere fancy. I wasn't sure where, maybe to breakfast or church.

My father wore a pair of gray slacks and a button-up blue shirt. The sleeves of his shirt revealed his form arms as the cuffs twisted up the arm; a mug in his hand with the overwhelming scent of strong coffee came from the room. My mom wore a knee-length, blue, and silver dress. Her hair was done up in a tight bun, and she also held a mug in her hand. I guessed that it was some type of tea as my mom didn't like coffee.

I walked forward to talk to my parents so I could speak to them about what they said. Josh stood behind me, and I felt his breath near my ear. Our parents were able to see both of us.

"Hey, Josh, why don't you and Mark stay for a bit?" Dad called out to us from the opposite end of the room we were at near the kitchen compared to the stairs, "We can catch up and finish discussing how Mark living with you will work. Since he'll just be staying with you but remaining under our guardianship, we will need to figure out how standards will be between the houses. We don't want Mark to forget the rules when he moves back in."

I stopped in the entranceway, not wanting to discuss anything. I didn't think I would ever want to move back unless Josh and George's become worse than this place. From what I had seen, that seemed very unlikely.

Josh spoke when he saw me leaving. He moved closer to our parents. "Could we do that later? I am tired from all the packing, and I think Mark is too. We can talk later if you want, but can I first drop all this stuff at my apartment?" Josh was looking at Dad. I couldn't see Josh's face, but his voice was quiet.

"Mark, we should go put these in the car and head out." Josh headed to the door, swinging it open, causing a slight bang. "Head to the car; I need to say some stuff to Mom and Dad." Josh's face was taut, and his eyes closed. His voice was quiet though I heard the words loud and clear. I rushed to do what Josh said, not wanting to see the explosion that I anticipated happening in a few moments. Josh's car beeped, and the lights went on and off, showing the car had unlocked. I ran, and I grabbed the handle of the door, closing it behind me as I ran out.

Opening the trunk, I placed my bags in the car and moved to the backseat. I kept my blankets, sensory tools, and drawing supplies with me. I curled up under one of my blankets and opened my art supplies. I started to sketch different art pieces using a new sketchbook of recycled paper. It was cloudy white with a few flecks of cream and had been a gift from one of my friends who learned to make paper. It was hand-bound in a spiral style and given to me to practice my art.

I opened the hard paper cover to see the new page of the sketchbook. This has been recently made based on what my friend told me had a thick paper quality, almost like watercolor paper. I pulled out a set of gel pens. Grabbing the blanket out the car window, I looked for something to draw. I settled on the old tree in front of our house. I traced an outline in a thick, black pen and began on the branches leading to the trunk in a thinner pen. Leaving behind spaces for the leaves, I carefully drew the tree, looking up every so often to check my drawing. The paper moved nicely as I worked, leaving behind no stretch marks or pierced paper. On the back, there was no bleed-through of the pens.

I had finished the start of the tree when I heard a slam. Looking up, I saw Josh heading toward me from our parent's house. His feet hit the ground, and if he had walked on loose dirt, I would have seen dust clouds. Josh appeared crouched over as he walked. His arms still held bags; Josh opened the trunk and placed the bags he carried inside the car, and there was a slam of the trunk. The driver's side door opened, and I saw Josh again. His face shaded red, and he breathed in and out deeply.

Turning around, Josh said. "Sorry about that. How about we head back to the apartment and then go to a shop of your choice? I didn't mean to take so long, but I needed to speak to our parents." He turned on the car engine, and we drove away.

The drive was surprisingly smooth compared to what I expected after the situation we had just left. Josh's face was still flushed, and his teeth gritted. I didn't know what Josh talked to my parents about, but I think he was angry about whatever they'd said. Reaching the apartment, Josh opened his door with a push and walked over to where I was. He grabbed the handle and opened the door, saying, "Let's go." I unbuckled the seatbelt and got out of the car, following Josh into the apartment building.

We walked up the stairs to the third-floor apartment. Josh pulled out his keys and unlocked the door. Josh pushed open the door and walked in. His feet made a thumping sound on the floor.

George sat on the couch. I still wanted to talk to him, but I wasn't sure how to start. "Welcome back, Josh. Is anything wrong?"

"Only my parents, George. I don't understand how I didn't see it sooner, but they just make me so upset." Josh's face still has a red tint, but on the drive over, he calmed down, and I faintly heard him saying Josh will help.

George turned to look at me and said, "Okay. Mark, how about you go to your room? I need to talk to Josh right now. Josh, come join me on the couch, and we can talk." George's body was turned around as he nodded to Josh.

Nodding my head, I moved toward the room I'd slept in last night. I added my bags to the others from last night. As I reached the door, I turned around and saw George and Josh sitting together on the couch, talking with their foreheads together. George's arms were around Josh.

Pulling out my drawing supplies, I think about what I wanted to draw to help me process. I finally decided to continue the drawing of Josh walking away from our old house with the tree out in front. I chose to draw the house in harsh and looming black and white lines behind Josh, looking like how I would whenever I would head in with the life being drawn out. The tree out front was grayscale to show life to me would return the further away from my parent's home I was.

Josh was walking, but his feet appeared to be covered, blocked by my car door. Long hair shaded his face. I drew Josh's outline in a harsh black pen, but his body's interior was done with a softer marker. His face was frowning as he walked away from the house, opposing the scale as he was in color compared to the house. I drew out the details of my hand resting on the window. Life and color left as the drawing near my parents' house. Monotone images closer to the house showed that life felt like it less whenever I would near the house. The house outline was in a hard black, with the interior windows in white. This showed the contrast between the interior and exterior. I was giving myself a clearer image of the rooms. My old room I did in a light color, and the rest of the house in black and white small outlines. The black and white outlined house loomed behind Josh as he left for the car's brighter, bright future.

My phone buzzed, so I turned it on to look at the clock and was surprised that it was around five in the evening. I had been so absorbed in my drawing that I hadn't even noticed how long it had been. Deciding to step out to learn what was for dinner, I saw Josh and George on the couch with their phones out and a text app open, but I couldn't make out what was on the screen. I closed the door exiting my room, though I guess I closed it a little too hard as a small slamming sound came out.

Josh and George turned to look at me. Josh smiled and spoke. "Hey, how about we go finish unloading and unpacking and then have dinner? George will come and help us. What do you want to eat?"

I nodded, and we headed down to the car to collect my items before heading up to unpack the boxes. I never answered what I wanted, as I wasn't sure.

We moved up and down the apartment building stairs, taking the boxes and bags to my room before heading back down to the car for another load. When we had left the house, I had my arms and back full of bags. Still, this time, we are only taking a few bags as there were multiple flights of stairs. We didn't want to get tired. The walk up and down the stairs was calm, though the unpacking was a monotonous task of moving items from my bags into piles before putting them away. As we unpacked, I grew lost in thought about the move and what was happening in my life: How I now had a new place to live that would hopefully feel like home to me.

I wanted to call Josh's apartment home and a place I could be safe and free where I had the chance to be myself. I took the final bag into my room, and now it was time to eat. Josh checked what I wanted to eat again. I honestly didn't care now, so I said, "Anything works." After that, Josh prepped a box of mac and cheese for us. This was one of the first times that Josh had prepared a meal specifically with what I had in mind. Normally, he would just make what he and my parents wanted, not really consulting me but just going off what I liked to eat when I was younger. The food tasted okay. Nothing was special or unique about it. Still, I enjoyed it since Josh had put effort into making what we were eating. This brought a smile to my face. I liked being able to eat with Josh again in a normal and happy manner.

After eating, I moved into the room Josh had given me, for now, to draw and potentially go to sleep. Though before I had a chance to draw, I crashed into bed and fell asleep with my socks still on. My brain craved sleep, and I couldn't focus any longer, and I went to sleep after an exhausting day.

Chapter Five

LEARNING WITH AN ALLY

Josh drove me away from the apartment to school. I had on a brown and black shirt with soft blue jeans. My bag was in between my legs as I rode in the car. I sat and waited for us to arrive at school. According to Josh, I was being dropped off at the school due to the apartment not being within walking distance as it was a few miles away which I guess was reasonable as we're a few miles from campus with no easy walking pathway to school.

The drive was quiet, and we listened to some music that I couldn't quite place who the artist was. We drove up to the school parking lot and met a long line of cars at the entrance. The car slid forward, and sunlight hit me in the eye.

As Josh pulled up to the school's front, I gave him a smile and said, "Goodbye." I got out with my bag and headed to meet Steve as we had planned. My feet hit the pavement, causing small shocks through my body. The sun warmed the back of my head as my hair shaded my eyes from the light reflecting off the glass and metal that made up the sides of the school. I smelled the flowers growing near the school though they had only a light floral scent.

Walking into the school was calm, as the hallways easily were able to fit a car or two going down them. While the building was big, the school population wasn't more than a few hundred. Walking down the hall, I saw many teachers and para-educators walking around, helping to take students to classrooms or talking with students who were new or had just transferred in. Para-educators help students who need more help, like one-on-one or in smaller classes. Many students and a few of the helpers wore sound-canceling headphones of various colors, causing a small, scattered rainbow to form if you look correctly. A few teachers were walking around with earplugs or headphones matching the students. Chewies swung around the necks of people as they walked, the rubber making a slight thumping sound. Glasses on people's faces scattered the halls: both regular and tinted. People's hands moved around with small fidgets. A couple of students' heads were down as they moved at the ground, only focusing on walking, along with letting their hands move around the fidget.

I walked to the art room and saw Steve standing outside. He appeared to be waiting for something terrible to happen.

I said to Steve. "How are you doing today?"

Steve turned to me and spoke, "I'm good. This is one of the first times I have been here by myself, so I didn't know what to do."

"That is fair. How about we head in, and I can show the sketch I have for your commission so far?" I had a smile on my face as we spoke. I loved to talk about my artwork and had fun talking with people when they understood how I could communicate.

"Okay, then let's head in." Smiling, I opened the door and walked into the room. Ms. Brown looked up at us from her desk and began to sign when she saw me.

Who is this, Mark? Ms. Brown tilted her head.

This is Steve, one of my friends. Ms. Brown, from what I knew, would be happy about this as she liked it when I brought in my friends or met them at my art sales. Ms. Brown loved to sign with my friend Valentine and had long discussions about art and life with them.

Okay, have fun. If you need anything, let me know. Ms. Brown smiled at us.

I will, Ms. Brown. I went to my usual spot and pulled out my sketchbook and sketching pencils to show Steve the drawing and work on the commission.

I pulled out the base sketch of the deer with the young child for Steve. It was rough to me, but I guess that Steve liked it as he stared intensely at the sketch. He then said, "This looks amazing, Mark. How long did this take you?"

I shrugged and said, "It's a quick sketch." I pulled out the shading tools in my bag, and I began expanding the drawing into a fuller-looking piece. Depending on how detailed I wanted to make it, this might take anywhere from a few minutes to a couple of hours.

The deer in the sketch bent down to eat some grass while a young child pets its head. It was done in a light pencil, so I would have the chance to do a harder line and then erase the light ones as I put on the finishing touches. I still had a lot of shading to do and would need to improve the size and shapes before giving it to Steve, but I think he would like it.

Steve's phone buzzed, and he let me know that we should start heading to our first class of the day. We headed out of the room as I followed behind him. We walked down the hallway together to see a few students moving into the hallway as we headed down the area enter another wing of the school. We reached the science area and headed to the door with our class inside. The room was full of chairs surrounding black surfaced tables. The chairs were computer-type rolling chairs made from hard plastic, but all wheels were able to lock in place. Steve and I sat down together.

The teacher stood in front with a sign language translator. The projector turned on in a light blue color with a welcome message up. The lights dimmed and then brightened to show that class was beginning.

Steve and I had been whispering until the lights dimmed. We got quiet and turned to the front of the room, awaiting instructions.

The instructor named Ms. Hill stood in the front, looking around with a smile on her face. The chemical hood was loud as it pulled up gasses from chemical reactions.

Ms. Hill moved forward and took the beakers from the nearby holder before calling us over to watch. Moving over to the hood, I put in my earplugs. Some of my fellow students had on headphones or colorful earplugs too. The teacher said she would show us electroplating with silver. Then we would move on to filling out the paper of safety procedures. She went through the procedure of mixing the chemicals safely, what to put into each beaker, and the methods of chemical and heat that we would be using to clean a penny. She apparently did stuff like this to get us interested in the project at the start of each section.

After the demonstration, we had to fill out the safety procedures before making golden pennies. That would be done with a different chemical reaction which would be shown again in the next class. Students helped to pass out pieces of paper to show we knew lab safety and remembered what to do after last week's presentation. Steve and I worked together to fill out the paper.

Steve's head went up, and he said, "How are you doing, Mark?"

"I'm doing okay. How are you?" I turned to Steve from the desk, so I wouldn't be mumbling into the paper.

"I'm doing okay. Do you want to meet up after school?" Looking over, I had a smile; we could hang out after school. This would be my first time making a new friend in my age group in a few years. I had Kyle and Sarah, but most of my friends were either my students in my art class or in college like Valentine.

I didn't know how to answer but that I might need to check with Josh first. I hoped my brother would agree. I decided to also ask what Steve thought we could do. I had a smile on my face.

"Couldn't tell you, Mark. If you want, there is the mall." Steve avoided my eyes, and his lips curved up.

"Okay, then let's go there. The mall has some stores and areas we could walk around in." I was excited to go to the mall with Steve and show him some of my favorite places.

"Sure, that works." Steve had a smile on his face. I was happy to see this and smiled back.

After we were done discussing the plan, we moved back to the worksheet. We traded back and forth, asking each other questions on the page. "What is the answer to this?" Question 13 confused me, so I asked Steve. *What do you put on your face to protect your eyes from chemicals and vapors?*

"I think it's safety goggles. Do you know what this is?" I pointed at question 7, which asked for a specific time to be given. *What do you do if you get chemicals in your eyes, and how long do you wash them for?*

Steve replied with "I think it's fifteen minutes."

"Thank you." I wrote down the answer before continuing the worksheet.

We continued filling out the sheet for most of the class. The teacher walked around to the different tables letting us know the class was almost over. For the deaf students, the interpreter tapped their shoulders and then signed that the class was nearly finished. This was done to get us in the habit of cleaning up before it was time to change classes when we were working with chemicals.

After turning in the paper, Steve asked, "How did your art sale go over the weekend?"

"It went great! How was your weekend?" I hoped that Steve had fun over the weekend.

"Busy. I had a lot of work to do at home and many chores. Sadly, my parents were too busy to drive me to your art sale." I thought that's what had happened. I was happy to know Steve remembered, even if he couldn't come to visit.

"That's fine; I still had fun. Though maybe I could see if my brother, if he's free, is able to pick you up for future sales." I hope Josh wouldn't view this as me overstepping, but I think he would be fine. If he said no, I would just need to say I knew he was busy.

"That would be great." Before I could respond, the lights dimmed, showing it was time to change classes. "Send me a text message for when you're available to head to the mall."

Chapter Six
UNSETTLING HISTORY

ENTERING THE CLASSROOM, I moved into my seat in history class. The teacher had a few different pieces of memorabilia from when they traveled. Mx. Linda was nonbinary and preferred to use they/them pronouns. Around the room were shields and mock spears with the edges dulled to a point where they wouldn't cut anyone. The light in the room was nice and calm, not too bright.

The teacher entered the room with a kind face. Their face was covered in slight wrinkles and clean-shaven with a couple of greying hairs looking like highlights. A PowerPoint was queued up on the screen. Our teacher uses they/ them pronouns as opposed to he/ him or she /her.

"Welcome, class. Today we will be talking about the recent changes happening to our city. As a reminder, I am Mx. (Mix) Linda. If you want, you can just call me Linda. If you need to leave today, you're welcome to do so, as today is a challenge by choice." The teacher passed out a class schedule. I saw a part in the projected class that I dreaded. It was about the major players in the actions that affected the city.

On the screen was a photo of the school before the changes. It had wide stairs leading up to the school. On the other side of the screen was an image of a ramp. The ramp had a railing leading up instead of stairs; this was the remodeled school.

"As you can see, the difference between the schools is that they have remodeled with ramps instead of stairs. You are some of the first students who have experienced this change in the school system. I would like to help you learn about all the changes and how they affected the city. This lesson will be over the next three class periods we have together," Mx. Linda said, pointing at the screen with a pointer.

The slide image changed suddenly and began randomly switching and changing slides. Mx. Linda moved over to their computer, face scrunched. "Sorry about this, class. I will work to get it fixed." They began to move around the mouse and click on different slides. I saw a few blurred pictures of various classrooms until the projector stopped on a blurred image. It appeared to be a protest like a few my parents had taken me to as a child. I didn't like being forced to go because the protests were always too loud. Mx. Linda messed around with the computer for a few minutes before finally turning off the projector. I was shaken but ready to continue with the lesson. My heart began to pound at the thought of my parents. I didn't know what to do, so I stayed and waited for the lesson to continue.

"Sorry about that, class. I think I got it fixed." Turning back on the projector, they showed the school's image again, yellow light tinting it now. "I guess that will have to do; let's continue the lesson."

The image changed again to show Mr. David speaking in front of a group of people. "Class, this is David; he is one of the art teachers in the area. Many of you might have had him in elementary school. He is well known in the area and volunteers at many different art programs. He fought for student rights in the school district. He helped make a new piece of art programming to help people with physical disabilities make different art. He worked on making a new program with the help of other teachers to recognize the body movement and sound for color. This program helps people to do various projects with just a camera and microphone."

The next image that popped up was the school board. Mx. Linda continued to talk. "This is where the schools started to change, due to teachers and parents campaigning about nine years ago. This helped jumpstart a new movement that is currently spreading through the area."

The next image appeared on the screen, showing schools being remodeled. "After this decision, the schools began to get remodeled, and many new people moved into the city. This helped to reinforce a need for what was happening. New families moved in when the city began becoming more accessible." The next image was of the city council from about seven years ago, with Mr. David standing before a group of teachers and parents.

"This is when the city began to shift with all that was happening at the school district level. Soon, the area was filled with special needs teachers, and new training began to happen for the adults." The next slide showed something I hoped wouldn't be brought up. It was the same image of protestors, but now I recognized the area. It was the same one my parents would protest in. I thought I saw my parents on the slide, but it was hard to tell as it was blurred to protect the protestors' identity.

"Not everyone was happy with the developments the city was going through. Many different groups were founded to fight against the changes, but they all failed. The groups claimed to be trying to help people by preventing 'fake disabilities from being accommodated.' This was false, as what they believed to be fake disabilities were actual disabilities."

The next slide showed an image of people walking around with picket signs in black and white, showing in their minds that there were only two sides. Over time, the groups in the pictures grew smaller until only a few people were left. Most often, it was my parent's remaining. I wasn't able to tell it was them due to how blurred the slides were, but I could recognize the names of a few of the groups they had founded. Why did my parents resist these changes to the city? The changes were fine and healthy, not wrong. My pounding heartbeat grew faster, and my head began to throb.

"These are a few of the groups who fought against the changes in the city and what it was going through."

My head ached at seeing the images. I was reminded of what my parents had done to me and some of my friends with their views. The lesson continued showing different pictures of the city, with explanations of what was happening. The lesson reached a part I had hoped wouldn't happen: one where they talked about the various groups, but luckily, no names came up.

"The groups that were founded started quickly but always fell apart. Many groups either moved away or left once they saw the benefits of becoming more accommodating. The city listened for feedback from the protestors but mostly ignored the hateful words around necessary accommodations." All that time Mom and Dad spent trying to create ways to prevent changes was either considered or ignored. My headache worsened as Mx. Linda, our teacher, continued to talk. The lights began to alter my senses. Words became distorted, and I stood up and ran. I fled the room, hoping the memories going through my head would vanish. I didn't want to remember what my parents had done. I wanted to forget the times I hated. I ran to where I hoped there was a form of help. I could get to the counseling center where Jaden should be working.

Chapter Seven

COUNSELING CRISIS

I RAN FORWARD, FOLLOWING the path to a counseling office that I barely knew, as I had only been to this office once at the start of school. My feet hit the ground, and tears streamed down my face from the pain in my head. My heart raced, causing a painful pounding in my chest. My cheeks flushed. Running into the mostly empty counseling center, I only saw staff, and I began to sign quickly.

I need Jaden. I need Jaden. I need Jaden. I need Jaden. My hands blurred as I signed, making them hard to understand, but the familiar motion was slightly comforting. I guess due to how much I was repeating the phrase, they understood what I was signing.

One of the people up front signed me. *Why do you need to see Jaden?* The person who was signing had their head tilted, looking at me. They signed slowly and repeated until I responded due to how much I was shaking and how often I closed my eyes. This person had worked with me in middle school before moving to high school last year. We talked, and they understood when I was like this to repeat the signs a few times to understand. The other option was for them to speak, but they wanted to keep to the same language.

I need help. I need help. Please let me see him. Please let me see Jaden. I closed my eyes and just began to repeat the same signs repeatedly about needing help and seeing Jaden. Someone opened the door and went into a back area. Eventually, the door opened, and Jaden came out.

"Mark, are you able to calm down? Is it okay if I touch you?" Jaden's voice was quiet and calm. He was used to this happening back when I was younger. I would freak out in class and run to the counseling center for help. I would have trouble with certain sounds that overwhelmed me. Or people would talk about a subject that made me uncomfortable, such as my parents' protests. I didn't like talking about those as they brought up memories and ideas I tried to bury. I didn't want to remember some of the words said about my friends at the time and how those might apply to me now. I couldn't handle it, so I would run away to places where I felt safe. Eventually,

I would end up at the counseling center or the art area where Jaden would be called.

I signed, *yes*, about his question of if he could touch me.

Jaden moved over and placed his hands on my shoulders, and I said, "Alright, I'm going to guide you to my office, Mark. We can talk there, okay?" Jaden's hands were light on my shoulders as he moved me around.

I followed Jaden back into the counseling center. My eyes were screwed shut, trying to keep the light from blaring into my eyes. My feet slammed into the ground, with me barely having the energy to lift them up fully. Sound shone into my ears, causing a loud sound and pain to spread through my body.

Jaden guided me with his gentle words and eased my frantic thoughts. He paused and swung open a door, leading me into a chair and lowering the lights.

"Mark, are you okay? How can I help you?" I barely heard what Jaden was saying. I just curled up into the chair, trying to shut down and reset. My legs pulled up to my head, my eyes covered my knees, and my arms wrapped around my legs. My head pounded, light glowing from somewhere blinding me into a state of pure white that turned dark as I squeezed my eyes shut. Sound blared again, and it was like I was in the middle of a tornado. The air conditioning was loud, the heater and the vent system were carrying sound from other areas. I didn't see what I could do but just sat and waited. I heard Jaden continuing to talk to me, offering any help in any capacity he was able to.

I continued to fold into myself and disappear into the comfy chair. I wanted to vanish and for all the thoughts I had about my parents to disappear. Why did this have to happen during my class? I had been fine, but now I wasn't okay anymore. I felt overwhelmed by my own head. I thought that I would have support, even though Jaden was right next to me. His words did not reach my rattled brain. I barely noticed that Jaden turned on some calm music; often, Jaden would do that for me in our sessions.

Slowly, I was calming down, losing the pain slightly, leaving it in the past. I moved my legs as they hung off the chair. I opened my eyes and saw a dark room. The lights were barely on, and the blinds were shut. Faintly was I able to make out what was around me from the light streaming in from the curtains. I sat in the spot, looking around, gaining my bearings. The lights brightened slightly until Jaden clearly appeared. The light was made to look like it was coming from behind grey clouds.

"Are you doing better?" Jaden stood next to the light switch with creased eyebrows and a look on his face I couldn't place.

"Yes. How are you?" I looked at Jaden with a smile that turned into a wince as the pain in my head returned slightly.

"I am good, but you gave me a scare. What happened?" Jaden moved back to his seat and looked at me for answers. He didn't look straight in my eyes, only in my direction. I'm happy Jaden knew my comfort levels and that I preferred to focus elsewhere with my eyes, so I was able to focus on what was being said.

"History. What does that look call?" I was curious; I had rarely seen such a look directed at me, and I forgot what it was called.

"It is called worry, Mark. What in your history class caused this?" It was a tough question for me to answer.

Should I talk about my parents and how they took me to those protests? I sighed and said, "The subject of the class. We were talking about the protests against the city changing."

"Thank you for trying to answer my question. I'm glad we have a starting place." Jaden was looking at me with a smile on his face. I didn't know how to respond, so I smiled back at Jaden. Not knowing what was expected was difficult, but now I could handle it. Jaden's face was kind. He looked like what I wanted my older brother to look like.

"Okay. What was it about the topic? Was it the images that were shown? I believe they should have been blurred, but it is still fine to leave. Those lessons are normally "challenge by choice." I know you would normally ask lots of questions in history in the past, as you enjoy the subject." Jaden was right; I did like history. I liked to learn about the past and how the world had changed, except when it got personal.

I said, "The teacher kind of brought up my parents. Not directly, but looking back, I recognized the groups they were a part of."

Jaden turned to me again with a smile, though his eyes were narrowed. Was he upset with me, or was he worried? "Okay, then. Do you want to talk about it?"

"Not really." My voice mumbled as I spoke.

"Okay, then what do you want to talk about? How can I make you feel better?" Jaden was still smiling, though he avoided my eyes.

"I don't know!" I said at a loud volume, my voice hoarse. I didn't know what to say. Why had I yelled at Jaden when he was only trying to help me? I curled up again into the chair to try and feel better.

"Hey, it's okay, Mark. I get it; you're upset, and you are allowed to yell in here. Would you like some food? I have a few granola bars in my desk drawer if you want since you're missing lunch. I can write you a note to go to your next class when you are ready."

I nodded my head to the offer, not trusting my voice or hands. Jaden handed over a honey granola bar, knowing I enjoyed that flavor. I ate the bar as we sat in silence, only my heavy breathing making any sound above a whisper. Jaden pulled out a weighted blanket and asked, "Would you like to use this until you are ready to return to your class?"

Nodding my head, I curled up with a star-covered blanket. My legs were together; my shoes kicked off. I stared off into the distance, letting the weight calm me down as I relaxed into the chair. Eventually, I felt ready and placed the blanket on the ground. I put on my shoes and smiled at Jaden. I signed *thank you* to him and turned to leave.

From behind me, I heard, "You are welcome. Please remember you are always welcome here."

"I know. Thank you. I'll see you later."

Chapter Eight

INFORMING AN ALLY

As I HEADED OUT of the counseling area, I took out my phone to see the time. I had missed part of the class by this point due to having a crisis. Walking down the empty hall, I looked around at walls and images I had barely seen before. I saw a poster advertising the local Queer Straight Alliance or QSA. The poster had a giant rainbow and a black and white background with information in an easy-to-read font.

Next to the poster was an advertisement for the local support groups and new ones made. The ground had a sparkle to it, and the metal classroom doors stood out in dark grey except for the ones that the teachers had decorated.

Continuing my way, I made it to the math formula-covered door that was the entrance to my math class. The door was covered in black and white formulas with a central rainbow ally tag. I opened the door and walked across the silent room to my desk. Ms. Mia's lecture had the class's attention, and I was able to slip in. The room walls were covered in different mathematic equations. They had a big classroom look even though the room was on the small side. The room was only able to fit around fifteen to twenty students if the desks were squished together.

I sat down, my head facing the screen, and saw shapes with equations next to them. Ms. Mia walked to my desk and handed me a packet of the shapes and equations. The class ended shortly, but Ms. Mia asked me to stay after class to talk.

"Mark, are you doing okay? I saw you were late to class."

"I am doing fine, Ms. Mia. I just needed to do something before I came to class."

Ms. Mia said, "Okay, I'm glad you are doing better. Remember, if you ever need to talk, the teachers are all here for you. Do you have a slip to excuse being tardy? If not, that's fine; just let me know what happened with the previous class so I can get in contact with your teacher." I held out the slip and gave it to Ms. Mia, saying I was at the counseling center. "Okay, thank you for this, Mark. Don't forget your backpack when you leave."

Heading out of Math class, I saw Steve standing next to the water fountain near my classroom. He was refilling his blue, see-through water bottle. He wore a black backpack with an empty water bottle holder. People were passing by, calmly talking and joking with friends. The rainbow of earbuds and headphones was forming in front of me. I was one of the last to leave the classroom due to talking to Ms. Mia. I went out in the hallway, trying to find Steve. Eyes trailed over the mass of students walking up and down, trying to find Steve. After looking over the crowd, I found him and walked over.

I tapped on his shoulder and smiled. "Hey, how are you?" I had a smile on my face. I was looking in his direction.

"I am good; how about you?" Steve's face had a grin.

I replied quickly, "I am doing okay." I really wasn't, and my voice quaked slightly.

"Do you want to talk about it?" Steve's face had what Jaden said was worried on it.

I wanted to change the subject, so I brought up the quickest way I could think of. "Not right now. So, where are we going?" I was looking forward to seeing what would happen, just happy to spend time with Steve.

"I was thinking of us heading out to the mall. Does that still work for you?" Steve's look of worry changed to one of caring.

I checked with Josh, and I could still go to the mall. I was excited for us to go. "How will we get there? Isn't it a few miles walk on the sidewalk from here?" I wondered if Steve's parents would pick us up or we would take the bus. It was slightly cold, but I enjoyed this type of weather. It wasn't too warm to go outside or too cold where I needed to wear multiple layers.

"I know a shortcut one of my friends showed me." Steve's grin turned into a broad smile. I was going to learn a new way of traveling through the city.

"Okay, then let's go." Exiting the school, we began to talk and walk.

"So, what classes did you have after science?" Steve had continued to walk while looking behind me.

I paused, thinking of my answer. I said, "I had history. How about you?" I wanted to distract Steve from what was causing him to worry about me by doing that. I didn't want him to worry when I had already talked things out with Jaden.

"I had P.E. How was History?" Steve asked again as we paused at a stoplight. I know Steve was doing what I would do if I was worried for a friend. I would try and talk roundabout that subject. Maybe Steve was trying to do the same. I still didn't want to talk about History class, so I thought of how to respond.

"Not the best." Wanting to move away from the subject, I asked: "How was P.E.?" The stoplight changed colors, and we crossed the street, continuing to talk. The conversation would often pause as we would stop to think about what to say.

"We learned a new martial arts form. I heard about a topic in history that was being taught today as we went over it yesterday. How did it go? I know I had some problems as some of my friends were against the change which happened. I'm here if you need to talk." I'm happy that Steve was there if I needed to talk to a friend. The leaves crunched under our feet as we walked down the sidewalk.

"Not right now, maybe later. What form did you learn?" I wondered about Steve's comments since I thought we had different teachers for History. I talked to Jaden earlier, so I didn't want to continue talking about it now unless I felt the need. Around us, some leaves fell from the trees, only to be swept away. They were like how I wanted these emotions and memories to be, though I knew that wasn't healthy.

"A simple one, based on a few moves we learned recently; it is hard to describe. So, I don't know what to say about it. I think I might be able to show you after I have finished learning the form. I guess it is like how art is for you; the process can be described, but it's not possible to show what art is. How has your art been?" Steve was slowing down from our fast-paced walk to a slower one.

Happy that we changed the subject so often, I said, "I've been practicing. I can show you some pictures later if you want." I enjoyed spending time with my friends and just being able to talk and have fun. The sun lowered in the sky and showed a shadowed path off to the right.

"That would be great. We need to turn here if we want to reach the shortcut." Steve had us turn behind the baseball field and led us on a small trail to a closed fence that wasn't locked. Opening the gate, Steve stepped through, and I followed. Closing the gate behind us, Steve led me to a small narrow dead-end street. "What should we do when we reach the mall? If need be, I can have my parents pick us up after we are done."

"Normally, I would look at the craft and game stores if you are okay with that." I hoped Steve would agree as I wanted to buy a few small crafts with the money I earned from the sale and put a few items on hold to pick up later. Afterward, I usually would return with a larger bag and in one of my friends' cars with their parent or guardian.

"Sure, that sounds great." Steve gave me a smile, and we continued to walk. I felt happy.

Chapter Nine

WALK WITH ALLY

CONTINUING TO WALK IN silence with only the sound of the wind, we reached the mall. Small talk popped up occasionally. We headed to the local craft store. It was a small mom-and-pop shop. Sometimes, I would get a discount from the people there because I purchased the supplies I used for my crafts. There were all kinds of craft and art supplies: fabric, colored pencils, paint, wood, glitter, scissors, sewing thread, glue, arts, craft blades, sketchbooks, and some chalk in the back.

We walked into the store that was small but filled to the breaking point; there were rows of ribbon wheels that filled the gaps between the fabric bolts, some with a pattern made in glitter and others with printed patterns. Each rack between the holders matched the colors in the section with varying widths. On one wall were different cuts of wood and pieces to be assembled. In the center was a small desk full of backing and a cutting table with a cash register. At the front were examples of different arts and crafts ideas. People could do with the store's supplies if they wanted—a few of the store displays I had made for the store in exchange for materials.

Steve turned to me and said, "This is a cool store. What should we do?"

"I was hoping to buy some new materials that I can pick up later." I thought Steve would be okay with doing this, but I didn't know. I didn't want to be judged by Steve for looking over different fabrics. I didn't think he was like that, but I remembered how my parents judged me for making various arts and crafts in my free time outside of school. I never told them I worked with textiles though I think they guessed based on seeing me bringing home bolts of fabric. They never commented, or maybe they missed it entirely.

"Okay, what are you looking for? I can try and help." Steve's feet bounced back and forth as he looked over the store.

"I'm trying to make some new rainbow pieces to sell." The city had changed to be more accepting of people on the queer people and pride, though many were still not as accepting, but I thought I could trust Steve. I was still questioning and talking to Valentine about my identity due to their experience helping others in the local clubs and school support groups.

"That's cool. I can't wait to see what you make." Steve's smile grew, and his bouncing increased.

"I can't wait to show you them when they are done." I was happy that Steve was interested in such pieces. I began to bounce and started to be happy and excited at the idea of us looking through the store together.

"What else are you trying to make?" Knowing that Steve was interested in what I was doing caused me to bounce more.

"A few animals pillows." I wanted to try a few harder sewing shapes and to make a simple-looking but hard-to-make pattern. I wasn't doing them to stand up on their own, so they would look soft and comfortable to cuddle with.

"Okay, I'll go and look for them." Steve moved to get different small fabric samples to show me. He returned with red, orange, yellow, green, blue, and purple colors. The colors ranged from dark to light, with even a few neon colors. I pointed at the dark and bright colors. I would use dark colors for a pillow and bright colors for lap blankets. Steve moved and put back the samples moving the fabric's bolts for me to go and get cut.

I smiled at Steve and said, "Thank you for the help."

"I had fun, Mark. What else are you looking for?" Steve turned his head to look around the area and see what else was offered.

I answered that I still needed some white thread and a few multi-colored buttons.

Steve responded that he would go look. We separated and moved around the store. I went and had the fabric cut. Looking over the counter, there were some metallic-looking plastic buttons; I saw Steve coming with a few different threads.

"Here is what I found." Steve held out some white thread and a few different thicknesses of the clear plastic thread. Pointing to the plain white thread, I moved to check out. We left the store with a few folds of fabric bought and some stuffing and binding, ready to be picked up later when I had bags or a car as I didn't want to walk around with that full of a bag.

Moving to leave, we moved to the local game store. It was run by a sweet couple a few years older than Josh. If I remember their names correctly, they're Jessie and Bethany. The two of them had been together for the past couple of years and worked together to set up this game shop. Jessie ran the counter and helped with product and management. If I remember correctly, Bethany worked as a game tester for the story. She would come to the local schools to give demonstrations and help the teachers learn how to incorporate games into the classroom. The couple has been a significant part of the community for the past few years as they brought in many board and card games. The two felt those were easier to teach though they also had a small video games section. They also helped to develop a new type of roleplaying system used with the school. It was designed to teach people how to interact in difficult social situations. The game focused on using a dice rolling system and turn-taking module to give an in-depth experience to the players. If the people would be playing wanted, it would either focus on the story being told by the person running the game called the Game Master or move around and switch between players. The goal was to help raise confidence and interaction skills in a safe environment to explore and learn.

The game store was bigger than the craft store, covered wall to wall, with shelves spanning the walls and filling the floor with tables and chairs. The shelves were full of games, ready to be taken home. There was a counter-off to the side with trading cards. Light covered the store similarly to the school: it was made to look like it was coming through cloud cover. This was obtained using filters over the glass and windows to make the room glow instead of harsh lights. Faint music played in the background creating a calming effect over the store.

Many long tables were blanketed with placemats of beautiful artwork. A wall of free-to-rent games stood behind the counter. If a person grew attached to a game they rented, it could be bought from the stores if the people playing the game like that copy or buy a new one. A few game consoles were scattered around the store with downloaded games on them.

Steve had turned around and asked me, "What are we looking for?"

"I don't know." I didn't like making choices of what to do. I preferred to let others make a choice when I didn't have a clear goal in mind.

"What do you normally do here?" Steve had turned around and was looking at the spot next to me.

"Look around for a game I like and see if it is for rent, then try to find people to play with me." That was what I normally did at the game store. I enjoyed playing games, but my school or art class friends usually couldn't play with me. Some of my oldest friends, who I normally spend the night with occasionally, Kyle and Sarah, couldn't join me for long after school as they had clubs. Valentine was busy with college and their job. Danny was too young to understand most of the games I currently liked to play. So were many of the people I worked with within the after-school club; I used to teach art to anyone who wanted to join—many of the people in that club I had become friends with.

Chapter Ten
DECISIONS ARE STRESSFUL

"OKAY, WHAT GAME DO you want to play?" Again, if I didn't know, I would usually spend a couple of minutes looking around before asking for a recommendation of what game I should try.

I replied with, "I don't know. I think I want to look at the artwork and then play a game." I did want to play a game, but I didn't want to pick one which Steve wouldn't like. I didn't want Steve to have a bad time with me as I wanted us to still be friends in the future.

"Okay, that works. Let's go with that plan. How about we find a game with some cool artwork to look over?"

Steve nodded to me and said, "Sure."

Steve came back with a small deck of cards. The game and art were simple and based on sea monsters. I smiled at Steve and said, "Let's play that." Steve had a smile, and we moved over to play the game on one of the play mats. Steve found a mat covered in an ocean with fish and monsters rising out of the water.

"Could we play here?" Steve was looking at me with a smile. The mat was smooth but had the option for hands to indent the surface to make picking up cards easier. Setting down the game, I sat on the opposite chair from Steve.

"Works for me." We sat down and began to play.

Steve set out the small board and the decks. The rule book sat next to him. We picked up the blue and black-backed cards and began to play. The game was evenly matched, and the text on the cards was larger than most of the essays I wrote for my English class or the texts we were required to read, making the text easy to read. As we played, the game got more intense, and Steve began to bounce in his chair. He started to list random facts about sea monsters that were printed on the cards. He knew where they were from and the myth behind many of the stories.

The game moved quickly, going back and forth as we grasped the rules. Steve's bouncing increased as his foot tapped. A smile covered his face as we bantered back and forth. Eventually, the game ended; both of us were smiling. Steve had won the game, but barely, as we had almost the same types of cards. We had built our own armies and moved back and forth as the game progressed.

"That was a fun game." Steve bounced up and down as he looked at the card before looking back up at me.

"I agree; thank you for playing with me." I nodded my head up and down, as it had been a while since I played a game with a friend, this time instead of a stranger.

"I had fun." Steve's bouncing had decreased slightly.

"Same. What should we do now?" I was glad Steve had a fun time, but I didn't know what to do now.

"I'm not sure; we could return the game to the counter?" Steve stood up and looked around.

I replied, "Okay." We headed up to the counter and returned the game. Steve pointed to a few sets of fancy playing cards. A few of them referenced different mythologies worldwide; others referenced a few popular tv shows and books. I was drawn to a mythology collection deck; fifty-four cards with different artwork instead of thirteen repeating images. This set had Greek, Egyptian, Norse, and Celtic deities and monsters used as the images.

"May we look at that box of cards?" Steve pointed to the box of cards I had been looking at. The store clerk pulled out the box and handed it over to Steve to look at while asking us to stay near the counter. The box was silver bronze with black lettering. Each side was created with a different set of symbols. On the back, it showed twelve cards in groups of three. "Do you want these cards, Mark?"

"I don't know. Maybe but I think that I should wait before I decide to buy them." I turned to Jessie and asked if she was able to put the deck of playing cards on hold until later.

Before Jessie could reply, Steve said, "I'll get them for you." A smile was on his face as he reached for his wallet.

"Steve, I can buy them later when I have the money and if I decide that I want them."

"No, it's okay. My parents gave me money to get you a gift to apologize for not taking me to your art sale. If there is something else you would like, I could get you that instead."

I sighed and nodded at that. At least Steve had a reason he wanted to get me these cards. I knew I wouldn't be able to argue based on what I knew of Steve. "Fine, but at least let me pay you back in some way."

Steve said with a smile, "It's okay. I can buy you this. I want to."

"No, it's not. I can pay you back." I didn't like being given stuff that I didn't earn, and I didn't feel I deserved this deck just because Steve's family was sorry. "You are still buying art from me anyway."

"Then give me a discount on that if you will feel better." Steve frowned slightly, and he continued in a different voice. It changed to one that I knew from when my students didn't get to do what they wanted. Steve insisted, "I can buy this for you now, and I want to."

"Alright, then, Steve, I will give you a discount." Steve handed the store clerk the money and gave me the box of cards. It was heavy in my hand but felt okay.

Chapter Eleven

MEETING THE SIBLING

WE HEADED OUT OF the game store, and Steve and I moved toward food. The bags we had from school and the fabric weighed us down slightly. We entered the food court and headed to "Mama's Home Cooked Pizza" to buy a few pieces of pizza. I looked down, and there was the small game Steve bought me, poking out of my bag. Steve told me he got the cards for me as he thought they could help me develop ideas for drawing or sewing and give us a game to play.

Entering the line to order food, we stood and waited. Both of us ordered two pieces of cheese pizza as we were hungry. Stepping onto a softer mat as we reached the area to pay for food, I ordered a sweet tea, and Steve ordered an unsweetened raspberry tea.

The people behind the bar handed us our pizza after we paid. We headed over to a table, and I saw Josh and George sitting together eating food. I saw them and wondered if I should go over and if Josh would like to meet them as I am still here. As I looked at them for a bit, their hands occasionally brushed each other, and they would smile and laugh. I wish Josh would talk to me more. I'm happy that he has such a close friend like George, but I want to know if they fully support me. Do they accept me for who I am without knowing all my identity?

"Who are you looking at, Mark?" Steve said, looking at my brother and George sitting together, having fun.

"My brother." As I lifted my finger to point at my brother, Steve turned and saw Josh, a smile growing on Steve's face.

Steve pointed at Josh, asking, "Who is he with?"

"His roommate." Though I guess he was also my roommate now too. I barely knew George, and I felt like I should be closer to him than I was for some reason.

"Hey, Mark." Josh was standing next to our table when I looked up at hearing his voice. His right hand was interlocked with George's. "How are you?" I looked over their hands and saw that they were close to each other. I wasn't sure how, but I think it was more than friends. I like how they had been treating me and working together to help make me comfortable.

My hands were full of pizza as I had started on my second slice.

Steve put down his pizza and said, "Hi, I'm Steve, one of Mark's friends." I was happy that Steve considered us friends.

Josh turned to Steve before and said, "Nice to meet you, Steve. I'm Mark's older brother Josh."

Steve had a smile on his face as he looked at the two of them. "How are you two doing? Also, thank you for letting Mark hang out with me."

George started to talk instead of Josh. "Hi, I'm George, and I live with Josh. I am doing fine. We came here because I recently moved to this area. I lived in the dorm apartments previously, and Josh offered to show me around. How are you doing?"

"I am doing good. Just showing George around to some of the places I used to frequent before going to college." Josh's voice was light and I think playful in his response. "How goes the mall? Are you having fun with your friend?"

"I am hanging out with Steve." My face was covered in a wide smile as I spoke, though a headache was starting to form from all the talking I had been doing. I pushed through it and continued to talk.

"That's cool. Do you need a ride somewhere?" Josh had a smile on his face.

"I don't know yet." Steve and I hadn't decided what to do yet.

Josh smiled at me and said, "Okay. If you do, just text or call me, and I can give you a ride."

I nodded my head with a smile and said, "Thank you."

"It's no problem. Well, George and I should get going. We still have a few errands left to run." Josh stood up and walked away, hands linked with George. We went back to get drink refills. It had been a few minutes since we had finished our pizza. We talked about where to go next. Eventually, we decided to just wander the mall and see what was around and any new shops we didn't know of.

The walk around the mall was fun as Steve showed me new places, such as a hidden away toy shop that apparently had great fidgets. We wandered around the toy shop to see if we were interested in getting anything. Eventually, we left to go and headed to the plaza.

"So, what do you want to do now?" Steve had turned to me. His eyes looked past my body, so we were both comfortable.

"I don't know." I hoped Steve had an idea so we could continue to hang out.

"Do you want to come to my house with me?" Steve's face had a small smile.

"Sure, let me just check with Josh before I agree."

"Can you call him?" Steve gave me a bright smile as he said that.

"I'll be right back." Stepping off to the side, I pressed on Josh's contact info and began the call. I was nervous. I preferred to text, but I can tolerate calling.

The call lasted less than a minute. The whole time I was moving back and forth. I occasionally flinched at the little bit of static filtering through the phone. Josh agreed to let me go to Steve's house and offered me a ride home if I needed one.

I walked back and reached Steve with a smile on my face. "Josh agreed to let me come over to your house. All I need to do is send him your address."

Steve asked for my phone, and I pulled up the text chat with Josh so Steve could enter the address. I handed over the open phone to him and waited for him to finish. After we sent off the text to Josh, we left the mall and began the walk to Steve's house.

The leaves crunched under our feet. Few green leaves remained on the trees, though a few brown leaves still clung to the branches. The walk was in silence for the most part until we reached the sidewalk on the other side of the mall's parking lot.

As we walked, we talked about meeting Josh and what Steve thought about him. How Josh seemed nice and that he would like to have a similar big sibling. Though he kind of already did, according to him, with the family he made with his friends. We talked about where Steve had lived. I found out he had moved around a lot as a kid and didn't remember all the places he had lived, except that they had been living here for five years. Steve also talked about his parents' aquarium and their programs after school for the local kids.

We talked about what teachers we'd had, and I found out he knew Mr. David. Steve loved the way that Mr. David taught and clearly remembered how kind and helpful he was when he would help teach his class in the grade up as Mr. David was a lower elementary school teacher and Steve moved here in fifth grade. How he would stop by and explain the concept when Steve was having trouble.

I bounced my head up and down as I walked. My hands swung around occasionally, and I returned my chewy when it fell out. It was in the shape of a shark's tooth and was made of light silicon for safe chewing. The road appeared to be a scattered color pallet ranging from bright colors and pastels to dark shades. It was interesting as we moved down the street. Some of the yards had various toys scattered around, and a few even had basketball hoops. We reached the end of the street. We paused in front of a red house with a gray roof. It was bright and easy to spot. A dark blue bike is covered in glow-in-the-dark fish stickers in the yard to make it easy to find.

In the front of the house was a lawn of grass and patches of blue and green flowers. In the front was a decorative bird fountain.

I said, "Your house looks great. I like the paint palette you have going on."

"Thank you. I would prefer blue, but it was painted this way, so it would be easy to spot at night since I get lost easily. I chose the fountain and a few of the flowers." We followed the concrete walkway to the door of the house. The door was a black and red swirl that I think was hand-painted.

Next to the door, I saw the dark blue bike covered in stickers. Steve brushed his hand against the bike's handlebars and seat as he moved to open the door. I used to do that when I would enter my bedroom to remind myself of where I was using nearby items that I would touch lightly. This was the first time I had been to a new friend's house in a few years since I had trouble making friends with people I didn't already know. I was bouncing up and down on the balls of my feet, ready to have some more fun and to be able to talk with Steve more.

Chapter Twelve

HEAD OVER TO ALLIES

STEVE PULLED OUT A set of keys on a lanyard covered in different sea animals and sea monsters. There was an image of a fish on the back of a key. As the door clicked open and we headed into the house, I noticed the design was like the layout in my parent's house. We moved from the landing entrance and up the stairs. We moved through a hallway with blue walls. Reaching a door, I saw a blue nameplate saying Steve. Steve's door was painted a dark blue and had stickers of sea monsters on it.

Steve opened the door and invited me in. The room was dark until Steve turned on the light next to the door; it wasn't a very bright light due to it being blocked by dark blue glass mixing with the bright white light. This made the room look like it was under a light film of water. I stepped inside his room which was painted to look like the deep ocean with dark blue water and a few bubbles rising to the top. On the ceiling was a distorted image of the starry sky painted like it was underwater. There were images of fish swimming along the sides of the room, and near the ceiling, the water grew lighter in color as if it were nearing the water's surface.

Around the room were many books on the ocean and stories of adventures involving the sea. I saw many different fantasy books on display on the shoulder-high blue shelves. On one side was an aquarium full of fish in a rainbow of colors. Next to the tank was a jar of fish food with stickers covering the plastic container. Under the aquarium stood a cabinet of the sea or ocean-themed games.

"I like your room." The room felt calm due to the light and colors.

"Thanks. So, what should we do?" Steve said, "I have some games we could play."

I looked around and tried to think of what game I might want to play before I said, "Which ones do you have?" I really wanted Steve to select for me as I did not want to decide, and I didn't want to pick a game he wouldn't enjoy.

Steve smiled at me and said, "There are many. Sorry, most of them are sea-themed."

Moving over, I saw a few homemade games peeking out behind the store-bought games being pulled out. The homemade games were laminated and stored in delivery boxes. Most of them were covered in different shades of blue and titles written in a handwritten scrawl. Steve pulled out a few homemade packs of flashcards full of images of sea animals. Next was a giant blue map in a tube.

Pointing to the rolled-up blue map in the tube, I asked what it was. I thought the game would be fun based on the look and the artwork.

Steve told me it was an old role-playing game made for him by his parents' employees and that all the art had been done by the team. It was a long sheet of butcher paper laminated with artwork glued to the board. The game was covered in different markings and had stains from old marker marks. Steve told me he had had the game since he was around eight years old. It was a homemade role-playing system using a single six-sided dice to play with.

I was glad that Steve had found friends and honorary siblings in his parent's workers. I knew I often made friends with anyone who would spend time with me, mostly teachers. Mr. David had helped as much as he could but never had I seen him spend so much time making a gift, especially one like this that is potentially fragile after all these years. Steve also talked about how the game had been given the same year that a few of his close friends had moved away. His parents and their colleagues at the aquarium hoped it would lift his spirits.

Steve unrolled the board in the center of his room. The map was covered in different paper rocks and images of monsters. Different tiles were shaped to fit into the board with monsters to fight, challenging obstacles, and blank areas to move through. It was a hexagon board with spots to place the tiles face down. The ground was uneven but was made with care. As I looked over the board, the artwork's quality and style differed in each hexagonal space. It seemed like people were given a set of hexagon tiles and told to do artwork that fit an ocean theme and then to place them down randomly.

I liked the look as it was homemade and created with care. Steve asked if I would like to play, and I said, "Yes." We began, pulling out a box of light and dark blue dice to play with.

"So, how do you play?" I turned to Steve for the answers as I was curious about what we would need to do.

"To start, you either choose or get a random character depending on which version you want to play if you want the easy or hard mode. On the side are the stats, and on the bottom is the effect. This is a cooperative game to reach the end of the game board safely on our ship. It will be harder to do with just two people, but it should be manageable." Steve pulled out a set of cards and gave me the one titled *Monster Fighter*. "That is one of the simpler characters to play, and it's one of my favorites. I enjoy fighting, but there needs to be a captain to play, which I will do as it is more complex, though I also love playing that character." Steve's face was covered with a smile, crawling around on his stomach as he reached over to grab pieces and set them up.

The cards appeared to look old and well used based on the paper, but the art was beautiful to look at. It appeared to be done in watercolor, while others were made in marker, pencil. I think I even saw a charcoal card. The one I had was of a captain standing on a wooden ship sailing over rough water.

As we played through the game, Steve listed facts about where the various cards came from and how the board was made. This was one of the first times. Recently, I had made a new friend my own age. I normally made friends with younger kids or adults. I was happy to spend time around someone new that was my age who I hadn't already known for over six years. Steve seemed very nice, and I was excited to continue being friends with him. I hoped he liked the art I was making for him so that it wouldn't hurt our friendship.

Finally, we reached the end of the board and finished the game. I was exhausted and fell to the floor, suddenly tired from all the thinking and talking we had done. I sat back up and began to sign.

Thank you for the game. I still wanted to hang out with Steve but wasn't sure what to do now.

Steve signed back; *You are welcome.*

I had fun. We should play this again. The game was unique and fun to play, different from other games I have played in the past.

I agree. Steve paused before signing back. *What should we do now?*

I am a bit hungry. I hoped that Steve had some food I could eat.

Steve signed back to me, *okay, how about we go and get some food from the kitchen?* Standing up, we left his room and headed down the stairs.

Chapter Thirteen
ALLIES OVERWHELMING

STEVE AND I WALKED downstairs until there was the sound of a TV in the background. I hadn't realized Steve's parents were home. I hoped they were okay with me being over as I'd never seen Steve pull out his phone to check. I didn't want to intrude in someone else's house without them knowing I was there. This was Steve's house, but I still didn't know what to do. I stood frozen in the middle of the stairs contemplating if I should run or not, so I wouldn't need to interact with Steve's parents.

Then I heard Steve yell something: "Hey Dad, Pa, I have a friend over. What is the plan for dinner? I am getting hungry, and so is Mark. He is the person who invited me to the art sale that he was working at."

Faintly from another room, I heard someone yell back, "Okay. We are having stir fry for dinner. Your Pa is currently making that. How about you two come down so I can meet your friend?"

"Okay, thanks, Dad." Steve then turned back to me with a smile and started to talk to me while motioning for me to follow him down. I followed behind cautiously as I didn't know these people, though I hoped they would accept who I was.

Reaching the bottom of the stairs, Steve led me to a different house area, and I heard something turn down in volume. Steve led me into a small cozy room with a couch and a TV playing an animated movie. A person sat on the couch and stood up. He was taller than Steve and me. We only stood around his chest to his shoulder area. He moved away from the cozy, deep red couch. He turned to the doorway I was standing in alone as Steve had walked forward, his arms out like he was looking for a hug, I think. I think Steve's dad bent down and embraced Steve for a minute before releasing, and he turned to me. "Hello, you must be Mark. Sorry, we couldn't take Steve to your sale last weekend. Hopefully, we can attend the next one whenever that is happening. So how has your day been, you two?"

Steve beamed, saying, "It was fun! We played the game you made with the rolled-up mat. It was fun. I hope we can play it again in the future." Steve began to bounce happily as he talked. "What type of stir fry is it, Dad?"

"We have shrimp stir fry." Steve's face began to spread an even larger smile as he looked at who I now knew to be his dad. I had yet to meet his Pa. "So, how was your day, Mark?"

I shifted back and forth before opening my mouth. "It was good."

Steve's dad smiled at me before telling me his name was Greg and introducing his partner, Steve's Pa, as Eric. Greg invited us to sit down around the small coffee table in the room to talk and possibly play a card game if we wished. Dinner was finishing cooking, and I was asked what time I should head back. I was told whenever I wished if it was before ten-thirty when Greg and Eric went to bed. I texted Josh asking if I could be picked up around ten. Josh said that would work, and he would see me then.

Steve pulled out a sea-themed deck of playing cards. We sat and played some simple card games as we waited for food. I didn't choose any, and it was mostly Greg who picked the games. Steve and I said yes to playing them.

After a couple of rounds, the three of us heard a call saying that food was ready. That came from Eric. Steve yelled back, "Thanks, Pa!" and we all stood up from our perches. I was sitting cross-legged, Steve was on his stomach, and Greg sat on the couch bent over so he could reach the table.

I walked behind Greg and Steve. As we entered the connecting room to the living room, we sat down at the table. It was meant to fit many more people than were in the house. It had a deep red room contrasting the dark blue outside of the house with gray siding and the floors. In the area between the kitchen and the dining room was a person standing there. He introduced himself as Eric. On his face was a smile as he looked out at me.

Steve bounded into the room; he turned to Eric with a smile and spoke, "Hey, Pa, this is Mark."

Eric had just set the pan of stir fry on the table and turned around to say, "That's good. I'm glad you had fun, Neptune."

Steve jumped at that name. I wasn't sure if it was positive or not. Steve frowned at his dad and said, "Thanks, Pa, but I thought we were working on coming up with a new name for you to call me." Around the room, I saw that Steve was in a blue stress ball chair. Many of my classmates had similar chairs when they worked as it helped them focus and let them bounce while sitting down, so they got to do that stim. I was in a regular folding chair. His parents were on the opposite side of the table with a pot in the middle with the stir fry.

Eric smiled at Steve and moved back into the kitchen while talking to us. "We are. You just haven't given me one yet. When you do, I'll change, or I could just call you Steve like your dad sometimes does." Eric gave Steve a nod and waited for a response.

Steve began to bounce on the stress ball chair he had at the table and smiled as he talked, "No, Neptune works, Pa. I like it. I just want to find a new name to fit, as that was chosen when I was like five."

Greg spoke and smiled at the two parties. "Steve, yes, you chose it when you were young, and you were first getting to know me, but that happened more around seven. That was when I first met you, and you wanted your Pa to have something special to call you."

I asked the question at the front of my mind as it seemed Greg had not always been a part of Steve's life. "So why did you choose the name Neptune, Steve?"

Steve looked at me. "That is hard to say. I don't really remember."

Eric said, "Steve, do you want your dads to share that story as you were young when it happened?"

Steve shrugged his shoulders while bouncing and said, "If they wanted to. I don't really care. I barely remember the story, so if they want to, they can."

Greg smiled at us and began to tell the story of what had happened. "You chose the name when I first came to be a part of the aquarium with your Pa, and you didn't like how close I was with him.

So, you and another one of the kids at the aquarium came up with nicknames based on your favorite myth, and you and your parents could call you that. Soon, all the employees got in on it by asking the kids they worked with for names and waiting for a response. I never got one of those nicknames until you were about ten and had started to accept me."

I gave Steve a smile and asked, "How do you decide who exactly gets a nickname?"

Steve remained quiet for a few moments before he shrugged in response. I guess Steve had forgotten the criteria. Neither of Steve's parents answered, so I guessed that they also didn't know what the criteria had been. Eric turned to me and asked how much food I would like. I only wanted a small portion as I wasn't that hungry due to eating pizza earlier.

I sat next to Steve in a regular chair while Steve was in a blue stress ball chair. His parents were on the opposite side of the table with a pot in the middle with the stir fry. When I had finished eating my meal, Steve motioned to me with a smile and invited me to show my artwork to his parents if I wanted. I wasn't sure why Steve was so excited about showing it to them. I pulled out my phone but kept it off, unsure if I should use my phone or pull out the sketchbook I had on me as I had some more finished pieces on my phone, but they could just look over my sketchbook.

Before I decided, Eric spoke up, "Mark, if you don't want to show us, that is fine. We are supportive either way." That didn't help, as that was like what my parents had said before they shot down my dream. I stood there, frozen, scared about what might happen. I didn't know what to do; I was caught in an unwanted situation.

Eric continued to reassure me when he saw how scared I was. "Mark, whatever your dream is, I am sure it is great. If you want to be an artist, that is great. If you want, you could even potentially help at the aquarium by making posters. Of course, you would be paid like all our artists, but it is up to you."

As Eric was talking, I began to unfreeze and hear and understand what was being said.

Steve then stepped forward and asked, "Mark, are you okay?" He was smiling at me and still bouncing, but his voice was shaky.

I nodded but remained silent, unable to talk. I continued sitting there, my phone clutched in my hand. I still didn't know what to do, so I sat there and let the encouragement flow over me. Their words helped slightly, but I still wasn't sure if my artwork would be up to their standards.

Chapter Fourteen

OVERWHELMED HEADING HOME

I CLOSED MY EYES and tried to take a few deep breaths to ground myself. I tried to focus on the smell of the stir fry we had just eaten. I listened to the breaths of the people around me. Faintly, I heard them ask if lowering the lights would help, and I nodded. The bright light dimmed as I sat there and tried to calm down so I wouldn't be so overwhelmed.

I moved my hand to grip the bottom of my shirt and moved my fingers over the textured fabric. I did the same with my phone case; as the rubber surface pulled at my skin, I repeated that action.

I continued to sit at the table, trying to calm down and to be able to talk again with Steve and his parents. Everyone remained quiet, and I kept my eyes closed, waiting to feel better. There wasn't much else to do while I was like this since my backpack was upstairs with my sunglasses and earplugs: my typical self-regulating tools. The grounding techniques I was taught by Jaden were working slightly but not as well as I had hoped. I tried focusing on my surroundings to keep my mind present.

My breathing became shaky again as I thought of what Steve's parents might be thinking and how I reacted to being asked to show my artwork. My hands began to quake as I tried to focus on what was happening around me instead of falling into a spiral of thought. But it was like I was failing. I wondered what Eric and Greg would think when I showed them what I had been making. My hand kept making the same repetitive motion over the textured items, even though my mind was spiraling.

It had also been years since I had been so overwhelmed that I shut down around strangers. I wasn't sure how they would feel about seeing me get so overwhelmed. I didn't know what to do but freeze. I wanted to show my artwork to them, but I wasn't sure how they would react, and I didn't want to risk getting the same experience as my parents.

I began to move inside my own mind and lose track of what was happening around me. I felt so small. Faintly, I barely heard Steve asking if there was any way to help, but I couldn't respond. My mind went blank, and my body felt frozen. I pulled my feet up to rest on the chair and tried to back up as far as possible so I could curl up.

I flashed through all the amazing moments I had shared with Steve, and I hoped that we could keep having those. I hoped that Steve's parents wouldn't disapprove of me. My mind came up with horrible situations before going blank and restarting with a new idea. None stayed, but they're still terrified me of what might happen. I preferred when the blankness kept me from thinking about what had caused this to happen in the first place.

I hoped that I could move and speak again soon to explain to them what had happened. I was scaring myself, pushing myself further away from reality, even when I tried to ground myself. If the last tether broke, I wasn't sure what would happen.

I forced my eyes open to see that shades had been lowered to cover the windows, and the room lights were turned off. Steve sat next to me, not making a sound. I began to blink as the pain had lessened though I had a massive headache.

I didn't know where Greg or Eric was, but I hoped they hadn't left Steve alone like my family did whenever this happened. My parents had always left me alone, left to hide away in pain.

Steve asked how I was when my eyes opened. He also asked if he could help me move to an area like the couch that might be better.

I tilted my head back and forth in an up and down fashion as I looked around, and Greg and Eric were standing in the kitchen. They moved over quietly and nodded at Steve. Steve asked if I could put my feet on the floor, so I was able to stand up. I moved my legs down one at a time, trying to adjust from their previous position.

We moved out of the dining room and into the room that Greg, Steve, and I had played cards in before. Steve walked slowly, letting me know how to move, so my eyes were able to remain closed. I followed Steve into another dark room and was guided to a soft couch my legs brushed up against. Steve moved me to the edge of the couch and said I could sit down in whatever position I wanted. I curled up again, and then I heard Steve and his parents talking quietly.

I began to feel better sitting on the soft couch, and I began to do the grounding techniques I had been taught. I opened my eyes; the dark blue walls of the room calmed me, and Steve talked faintly in the background. I didn't know what was being said, but the reminder that I had a friend nearby was helping.

This scene was different from what I was used to when I'd become overwhelmed and with someone who didn't really know me. The last time this happened, the people I tried to become friends with left me alone. I'd tried to find them again, but I felt tense around them. We still talked, but we weren't as close as we might have been.

I tried to listen to what was happening around me instead of just listening to the calming sounds. I heard them talking about the aquarium and how they had sensory days. That Steve was glad, his parents had the training to help with this situation and understood what was happening.

I tried to chime into the conversation, but my voice came out more like a croak. Steve and his parents still heard me, and the group turned to smile at me.

"Hey, Mark. Are you doing better?" Steve moved closer to me, though he didn't reach out to offer any physical comfort. It was nice to know that I had support around me.

I nodded with a small smile. I began to rock back and forth on the couch, almost ready to talk, though my throat still felt slightly off. I took in a few deep breaths, trying to clear my throat of the weird itch in it.

Eric spoke up in a calm voice, asking if I needed anything. I thought for a few moments and felt that the answer was no, so I shook my head. Eric nodded and moved to another chair to sit down. Greg did the same. I wiggled my toes and shook my feet back and forth, twisting and moving them randomly.

Eric smiled at me and began to talk about the aquarium that they ran. This was a distraction from what was happening. I just let him talk and responded only when I had a question. The topic of nicknames and how they spread around the place was a fun story.

Eric talked about how the workers would often bring their children to the aquarium after school. They had partnered with many local businesses and surrounding areas to offer a career exploring program after school. This was designed to help people with various needs or abilities learn about options available to them if they tried. The groups made the program as accessible as possible for the town and modified or changed the program if new details arose. There were always different types of programs for different groups.

The program at the aquarium ran every weekday except for national holidays and had various levels that let everyone interact together as a group before splitting off into their chosen fields for that week. There was limited space, so waitlists were made, but each kid normally got to do their favorite exploration every month.

We talked back and forth about how this all worked and how nicknames formed. They apparently started to confuse people with the same or similar first names and spiraled from there until everyone in the program had a name. Steve was one of the first, along with his other friend Steven. Steve got the name Neptune, and Steven was given the name Achelous. The two of them had apparently gone over a list of over a thousand names and picked their favorite name out of a list of water deities.

Chapter Fifteen
GET CLOSE WITH SUPPORTING FAMILY

Apparently, everyone in the program knew each other through the aquarium and first met each other there. This was the start of a tradition at the aquarium. People would pick a name they liked from a collection of water deities from many regions and myths. But for the employees, the people in the program would choose the name they got. No one was forced to have a nickname, though, and they might still go by their first name if they wanted. The workers made it clear that people in the program could go by whatever name they wished.

I wish that I had fun stories like this with my own family, but I didn't. I had some with other people, but not really with my mom and dad. Though Josh did try when I was younger, he returned from college at the start of each summer.

As Eric told the stories, Steve interrupted and added his own version of what he remembered even though he had been young. I wish I had that level of confidence to interrupt my dad when he talked. I never knew what to say when we talked since we had such different opinions.

After Eric finished talking, I felt better and started bouncing and rocking happily on the couch. I was no longer shaky about moving around and asked Steve if we could go to his bedroom, so I was able to grab my backpack to show Greg and Eric my sketchbook. Steve nodded, and we headed up the stairs to grab my bag.

When we got back, I settled onto the floor as I wanted comfort without the risk of possibly falling off a chair. I reached into my backpack and pulled out my sketchbook. It was black and covered in gold and silver marker in a scribbled design of mostly loops and zigzags. Before I opened the book, I sighed over the book before I said, "I hope you like what I made. I'm sorry about earlier that normally doesn't happen." After waiting a few moments and with some encouraging nods from Steve, I flipped open the book. I tried to think about what I should show them, and I landed on a simple landscape sketch I had done a few weeks ago.

I showed some practice sketches from a graphic novel I was making with Valentine and some small sketches of my surroundings in different places. These weren't very big, only small thumbnail sketches about 3x4 inches. However, they still apparently had more detail than Greg and Eric were used to seeing from simple sketches. I hesitantly asked if they wanted me to draw anything for them as a thank you for having me over. For some reason, they said no, but they did ask if I did custom projects. I nodded and explained that I would need to know more about the project before giving a price. Eric and Greg nodded, saying they would be in touch with me about that.

I continued to flip through my sketchbook, giving encouragement I had never gotten from my own parents. This was hard to do and explain what was happening in the image and my future. I hadn't really shown my artwork to people I didn't know very well. I had a connection with Steve, but I wasn't sure how I felt about his parents. I didn't know them as well as Steve, and while I trust adults, some of them are not the kindest and don't accept my chosen path of being an artist. I showed the rest of what I viewed as my complete sketches, barely focusing on my pieces and skipping over some that I hadn't finished yet or were personal commissions.

After I had finished showing my drawings, Eric asked me if there was a possibility for me to do a commission for the aquarium about their after-school program. I was shocked that they would trust me with such a project. I exchanged phone numbers with them so I could schedule a meeting to discuss the plans.

After talking about commissioning and what would happen next, we moved on to playing a card game. We switched games, often pausing partway through to talk about what was happening and how we should move forward.

We heard a knock at the door. I sat on the floor again at the low coffee table with a stomach full of stir fry. Moving up off the couch, Eric went over to the door and answered it.

"Mark, your brother is here to pick you up." I got up from the table and gave my cards to Steve to be shuffled back into the deck. Josh stood in the doorway, wearing a brown coat with the hood up. I grabbed my backpack and looked back at Steve and his family. I saw a family I wish I had when I was first criticized for doing artwork. I viewed Steve's family as one who would support their child in whatever he wanted to do.

Steve stood up, walked over to me, and gave me a smile. "Thank you for playing games and coming over with me today. I had fun."

I gave them a nod and said, "It was fun. I hope we can do this again. The food was good, and I had a great time."

From the living room where we had been until Josh had come, I heard I think Eric tell me, "You are welcome over whenever you wish. I hope you had fun and have a fun night."

I called back into the house. "Thank you." I then looked back at Steve and said, "Thanks for the fun day. Talk with you later?"

"That would be great. I'll see you later." Steve turned back into the house and walked back to his family, and I walked out to Josh's car and closed the door behind me. Steve wanted to run his family's aquarium when he grew up and finished college. His parents offered him full support by letting him decorate his room however he wished. Steve's parents were nice, and I wished I had parents like that. I hoped Josh would be as supportive of me as Steve's parents were of him. As I reached the car, George was sitting in the passenger seat.

As I got in, George turned around and asked, "Hey, Mark, did you have fun with your friend?"

"It was fun. We played some games." I had enjoyed my time at Steve's house. The games we played were fun and gave me joy.

Josh opened the driver's side door and began to talk to me. "Did you have dinner, Mark?"

"Yes, I did. We had stir fry."

"That's good. How about we head home and get some sleep? We can continue to pack up tomorrow after school." Josh looked back at me.

I signed *yes.* Josh drives away from Steve's house, back to his apartment and my new home.

Chapter Sixteen

SKETCHING HELP

Waking up in the morning was challenging, but I managed to get dressed and eat some honey cereal before school. Josh drove me to school and let me know that he would pick me up after school. Walking in, I saw the sea of students starting to form as I arrived later than usual.

Walking through the hallway, occasionally dodging a student or teacher with a cart, I reached my art class. The door was open, and a few students inside the room were working on projects. Ms. Brown sat at her desk, ready to teach. Her projector was turned on, showing some papers laid on top of each other. The papers were face down, so I couldn't see what had been drawn. I walked over and got out my weaving for the day to try and finish last week's project.

I also pulled out my sketchbook to continue the sketch Steve had commissioned of the deer. I'd worked on it last night and this morning and was almost ready to show Steve. The sketchbook also contained drawings for the graphic novel I was creating. The work was tedious but rewarding. I loved to draw, and by working on the story in my free time with Valentine, our friendship grew closer. I wanted to get Ms. Brown's opinion of the drawings and how I could improve them. Often, Valentine told me that they looked good and didn't need to change, but I wanted to get some unbiased feedback. I began to weave the brown and green yarn in my loom until the lights dimmed and other art teachers began speaking to us while Ms. Brown signed in front of the class.

"Hello, class. Welcome to our second week together today. You can either continue working on your approved project or learn a new technique." I would often look up and look at Ms. Brown, signing out the instructions and the slides with more information. I just wanted to listen and work on my project without stopping. "Today, I will be showing you how to do three-dimensional art on a two-dimensional plane. If you already know this, please, help a fellow classmate if they're having trouble." Nodding my head to the idea of helping others, I waited as the class went on to teach people how to do the technique. I continued to do my project, but I occasionally looked up to see if anyone needed help.

I have already used this technique often in my artwork due to commissioned pieces. Ms. Brown showed a simple way to make art appear to be in a three-dimensional space on the projector while signing what she was doing. The other art teacher spoke aloud about what was explained to the students who didn't know sign language. I continued weaving until the other art teacher speaking for Ms. Brown and giving the same lesson stopped talking. He said that it was okay to move on to practicing on our projects. We could incorporate the new technique in our future projects if we wanted to. Looking up from my weaving, I saw people practicing together.

Walking up to the front of the classroom with my sketchbook in hand, I tapped on Ms. Brown's shoulder. She looked up at me and smiled before signing, *hello, Mark, how are you?*

I smiled and signed back. *I am good. Would you be willing to look at some of the sketches for the graphic novel I am making?* I hoped she would say yes to my request.

Sure, do you have them with you? I was glad that Ms. Brown was willing to help me with non-school endeavors.

Nodding my head, I held up the sketchbook. Opening it to a bookmarked page, I showed the pages to Ms. Brown and waited for her thoughts. The first page had four blocks of images. One was a smiling wolf. The next block was of a young child moving into the area with the wolf. The third image was a boy standing in front of the wolf, looking on in wonder at the large wolf, his fingers sticking out. In the final image, the boy's hand was lowered, and he was petting the smiling wolf.

I looked at her and signed, asking, what *do you think?*

Ms. Brown smiled before she asked me a question. *These look nice. What perspective are you drawing it from?*

I thought for a few moments before I replied. *I was trying to do the first person for these images.*

Ms. Brown then signed back to me, *okay, then this works. The hand being held out helps to show that. I like how you use the perspective to your advantage with the hand.*

I gave her a smile and nodded before signing, *Thank you. Is there anything I can do to improve the piece?*

Possibly shade in with ink so it won't smudge as much. Other than that, it looks good. Ms. Brown was good at giving information on how to improve artwork like this. She used to work in a similar style.

Okay, I will try that. Walking back to my table, I put away my sketchbook and continued my weaving project. I saw a few people in the room who were having trouble with the perspective lesson. I remembered that those of us who already knew the technique were asked to go around and help others if we could. After finishing the row, I made it look like grass at the edge of a lake; I stood up and walked over to one of my classmates. I think her name was Sophie.

Tapping on her shoulder, she turned around and looked at me for a moment and said, "Hello, Mark. Do you need anything?" She then turned back to the image and frowned.

"No, I just wanted to see if you needed any help." Sophie was trying to turn a few squares and rectangles into boxes and crates. By taking the points to the horizon line, her drawing worked, but the lines weren't as clean as they could be, and it was clear that she was holding the ruler wrong.

"I think I want to figure this out on my own, but if I need any help, I'll ask. I am practicing working on the technique. I should hopefully know how to do it by the end of the day." Sophie looked up at me with a smile before going back to drawing a table.

I walked back to my desk and continued my weaving project. Occasionally, when my hands would start hurting, I would get up and check if anyone needed help. If they did, I gave instructions on what to do and how I learned to do this technique from watching videos.

After walking around the classroom and working on my own project, the lights started to dim, and it was time to pack up. I put away my art supplies in my locker and headed to the gym.

My classes for the day were Art, P.E., and English. I wanted to sleep or draw all day, but I needed to pay attention to my classes.

I walked into P.E. and was told to do some stretches to warm up my muscles before doing four laps around the track. Today's schedule showed a day of group yoga. This happened every two weeks so we could learn about our classmates and ways to calm down. Today, we would be doing breathing methods and simple yoga.

I sat down on the ground and stretched out my legs. I moved my legs apart and back together. I reached my arms toward my toes and held for around 15 seconds until I started to get tired of the stretch. Once I finished all the stretches on the ground that I knew, I stood up and stretched out my arms, neck, and shoulders. I was one of the first done stretching as I was fit and sometimes stretched for fun. I began to walk around the track at a quick-paced walk.

This was a quarter-mile track, so we would be doing one mile today for the warm-up. I continued my walk around the track at a slower pace as I wasn't feeling up to going too fast today. The track was a newer rubber one and, for the most part, smooth before leading into the football and soccer field.

I completed my first lap, getting lost in thought around the plot of the story I was helping craft with my friend Valentine. I had just finished the most recent chapter of my graphic novel, and Valentine had just finished writing the story. All that was left was revisions before I finished the drawings and added dialogue. The major scenes had been drawn already. Valentine had already fully revised those parts and had started to edit the story in the major plot points.

I needed to finish the final design of the wolf and correct all the signs where sign language was used. The story focused on a few characters, but I wanted to show the perspective of one character that was mostly off to the side but in each of the major parts of the story. I had the story shown from his perspective and had Valentine type out an explanation for how the art would look and why I had written it in such a way.

I preferred first-person artwork, so a viewer knew where the image was coming from. I neared the end of my third lap as I thought about the next part of the story. The action scenes caused some problems for me and gave me some trouble due to me not being the best at drawing those, but I knew I would get through this and finish the project. The next scene to draw was an active part of the group running away together through the woods. It has many interesting angles to draw from, especially from the character's perspective on the side of the action.

One of the PE instructors whistled. This was to signal those who, like me, got lost in thought. We were to stop walking and do the cool-down exercises. I sat down on the ground to stretch some more and waited for my classmates to finish their laps around the track. When I felt well-stretched and no longer tired from the laps, I stood up and moved over to where one of the teachers talked about today's plan.

"Hello," I said to the instructor. I think his name was Mr. Chris.

Mr. Chris replied, "Hi, you're Mark, correct?" I nodded my head and asked for his name. He said I could call him Mr. Chris. We talked for a few minutes together about martial arts, as he was one of the instructors. He had an impressive time for a walking mile and said that he was the Jujitsu instructor for the school. The rest of the group finished after a few minutes. I loved to walk around and get lost in thought, but I was ready to move on to a different activity.

The classes moved from the track up to the gym. Heading inside, we pulled out mats and laid them out on the floor to get ready for yoga.

We went into many different beginner positions and practiced breathing. This was very relaxing to do and was making me relaxed from the quiet and just breathing.

We finished when a timer went off from Mr. Chris's phone. We were told to go and change for lunch. I hoped I could meet up with Steve again.

Chapter Seventeen
BREAK WITH ALLIES

I PULLED OUT MY phone and sent a quick text to Steve, asking if he wanted lunch together. He quickly texted back, said sure, and asked me to meet him in front of the cafeteria.

Walking through the crowd of students, I reached the front of the cafeteria and put in my earplugs while I waited for Steve. The area was loud and hard to hear, but I was prepared for this with my earplugs. A fog began to cover my mind showing I was starting to get overwhelmed until I heard Steve's voice. We stood in the crowded area of students before we started to move to one of the quiet, mostly empty hallways.

Walking away from the cafeteria's crowded area, we reached a side hallway that wasn't very crowded and sat down to eat. Pulling out my packed lunch, I saw Steve doing the same. I had made myself a cheese and ham sandwich and packed a water bottle with a packet of raspberry tea flavoring. Steve pulled out a sandwich. This one had peanut butter and jelly and a bottle of juice, along with a bag of potato chips and a small cup of Jell-O.

"So, how were classes today, Mark?" Steve asked me.

"They've been good so far. I only have English left, and then I leave to go with my brother to my parents." I wasn't excited to be going back, but I knew that I needed to pack up my room to finish moving over to Josh's. I couldn't move out entirely as Josh's place didn't have room for all my stuff, but I was excited to be out of their house.

"Cool, I enjoy that class. I wish I had it last. I really enjoy that class. So, your brother is picking you up?" Steve still had his head tilted as he asked the question.

"Yes, he is picking me up. We are going to go back to our parent's house to continue packing." Why did I have to say that? I guess I'm just comfortable around Steve. I didn't want to hide from my new friend what was happening.

"Are you moving, Mark?" Steve turned to look directly at me.

"Yes. I moved in with my brother." I hoped he wouldn't ask why. I didn't want to tell him what was happening at home and how my parents didn't accept me.

"It's cool that your brother is letting you move in. Which are you going to call home: Josh's place or your parents?" It was a fair question, although it was still hard for me to answer.

"Currently, I feel more at home with my brother, but I'm not sure yet." I truly felt more like my brother's place was home. Still, it was hard to not consider the place I'd lived in for years to still be home.

"Okay. So, who do you have for English?" Why was Steve asking so many questions? At least he was changing the topic.

"I mostly work with Mr. Cameron. He lets me draw out my thoughts so I can remember what we read better." I truly did love drawing. "Do you ever work with him?" I knew that Mr. Cameron would sometimes go and help others at the request of the other teachers. In my opinion, Mr. Cameron explained the topic differently and better than some of the other teachers I had.

Steve said, "I sometimes work with him, though only when I have trouble coming up with ideas. He helps me think of the story, and we read in different ways. He asks us to describe what's happening in the story in our own words so we understand it better and can share it with him and the class." I liked that we both worked with Mr. Cameron and had similar teachers and classes to talk about. We could possibly do some homework together too.

I replied, "Yeah, Mr. Cameron is great. I love his teaching style. He is so free form and lets us work on different types of programs. I don't know how he grades all of the work as quickly as he does." Mr. Cameron would grade all our work within a week or two of us handing it in. Most teachers got the work back to us within a few weeks, but Mr. Cameron was consistent and always gave feedback on our work.

"I wish some of my teachers were more like that. How is your art class?" Our conversation was pleasant, making me confident in my decision to befriend Steve.

"Currently, I am working on making a new type of spiral weave mixed with a straight weave. How are your classes, Steve?"

"They are great. I have English with Ms. Nat. She is very nice and helpful. She uses a volunteer reading scenario to try and give us the courage to read to the class or even just sign while the interpreter translates. We can even just write down the passage and have another student read it aloud if we want." I liked how the school had sign language interpreters for the classes. The students were integrated with each other or a student like me who sometimes prefers using sign language. We also had a few deaf instructors or hard-of-hearing teachers, so having the interpreters helped make classes work better together. "That's cool of your teacher, though I think I still preferred Mr. Cameron."

I continued my line of questions with, "What other classes do you have that you enjoy?"

"The only other one I can think of is P.E. because I can run around and exercise in a fun way that actually interests me. I am normally very energetic. If I can get out my energy early by exercising, I can focus later in the day."

"I agree P.E. is great. Though I prefer art as I can do more." Since I loved to draw and create art and crafts for others to see, I wanted people to take my work home with them. With martial arts and the exercises in P.E., people only were able to take home memories.

Steve asked, "How is artwork going, Mark? Are you having fun with the art I commissioned?"

"It's going. I have been drawing and practicing, mostly trying to get my forms to a high quality and make sure I build up muscle memory with them. I have been doing exercises to help me learn to draw a straight line free-handed. I am hoping to do some more work on my graphic novel over the weekend. I have been working on your commission, and it comes along. I should hopefully be done in a few days to a week if everything goes to plan." I hoped to complete the scenes I was thinking about in P.E. over the weekend or get a start on them.

Steve's face grew a grin, and he turned around to me with a smile, asking, "What is the novel about?"

How should I explain the novel without spoiling the plot? I guess I couldn't, really, as the main descriptions would give away too much of the story. "It's hard to say without ruining the plot. I can say it uses a lot of sign language and works to show different cultures along with the difficulties people face while going through their life with a disability." I hoped Steve would accept that explanation, as I didn't want to spoil a story that was still in revision.

Steve kept his smile and said, "That sounds cool. Let me know when it gets published."

I was happy that Steve accepted my explanation. "Will do. How are your parents doing?"

"They are doing okay, working in the aquarium and letting me help with some of the work, such as feeding a few animals. If you want, we could take you and Josh over some time."

I'd already met Steve's parents, but him wanting to bring me over to where they worked felt exciting. I hoped Josh would agree.

I said, "Sure, I'll ask him?"

Steve nodded his head and replied, "I hope you can visit soon."

Eating food with a friend during school was nice. Normally, I didn't have this with Kyle needed or Sarah as they had clubs or were with another friend. I would normally eat alone, work on my art, and do small sketches to help me remember what we were taught. I found I learned better by seeing or hearing rather than reading. So, I would most likely forget what I read anyway. That is why I am glad Mr. Cameron also gives us an audio version of the stories we read to remember what was read about. I would also sketch out the images from the story as I listened to help me remember.

We ate our sandwiches and sat in comfortable silence. Occasionally, we sipped our juices as we ate our food. Eventually, the lights began to dim, and it was time for me to head to English and Steve to P.E.

Chapter Eighteen
DRAWING A STORY

STEVE AND I BEGAN to walk to our classes with smiles on our faces. I was happy about being able to eat lunch with Steve and walk to class together. Moving through the hallways, we reached Steve's class first and went our separate ways. I walked down the hallway to my class. I will be working with Mr. Cameron today on reading a story. I'm not sure what we would be reading, but I was excited as he always picked interesting short stories or excerpts from the writing; he lets us choose what to read.

I entered the classroom and went to my section of desks where Mr. Cameron was sitting and waiting for me and the other few to arrive. On a couple of desks in our classroom section were small packets for us to read through or listen to Mr. Cameron read if we so chose. He would record the readings in an audio file to listen to online using the school's website. This was to make it easier for each style of learning in class to be able to learn. I could listen and draw instead of focusing on reading the whole time and not being able to draw.

When the lights dimmed and everyone was in their seats, Mr. Cameron started the lesson. "Welcome, class. How are you all doing?" We all answered that we were doing good, okay, or tired, but no one said they had a bad day. Mr. Cameron nodded at the responses and said, "Today, we will be going over a new story called 'No Vision.' This isn't our normal type of story for this term, though. This is one that I wrote as an example of writing for us to examine and look over. It is flash fiction, so we should have plenty of time to review the elements after reading or listening to the story. This will be an introduction to one of the main ideas of this semester. You will be required to make your own story based on an idea we have gone over this term either in writing or drawing, and what we will be going over today is an example of that." Mr. Cameron paused in his talking before pointing to Jasmine, one of the students in our small group.

"Mr. Cameron, what is it about? How is it different from what we read?" Jasmine looked at Mr. Cameron with what, I think what a questioning look based on what she said was.

"That's hard to say, but it mostly varies in the fact that it has very little dialogue and mostly focuses on description to get the story's meaning across. We have been reading recently mostly using setting and dialogue to tell the story, not mostly setting and context, so that is one difference. The dialogue could be removed from this story. The meaning would stay mostly the same." Most of the class looked like they understood that, but some were not as sure. Still, we were told that after reading or listening, it would be easier to understand. "Now pick your medium, forgetting to know the reading, and we can move on from there."

I pulled out my phone and headphone and listened to the track put onto our school's website for us to listen to in class. Before pressing play, I pulled out my sketch pad and drawing material to use as I listened to understand the reading better. I listened to the reading about a trapped person who views the person trapped as a brother who tries to free them. I began to draw out what I heard, occasionally pausing and rewinding to listen again to certain parts to get the whole story and understand what was happening.

I drew out a cylinder with a person descending from it to the ground and another person in red standing by watching this happen. I showed a hallway leading out and drew this diagonally to show the two points of view being given from one character. I drew out the details in the first scene before moving on to the details given in the story. I drew a faint outline of hangar doors in the background as described at the end of the story, slowly opening. I had wind from the doors moving and blowing into the room with the story's focus, the two supposed brothers. I left the skin tones ambiguous as that was never stated in the story, so I only showed the characters' outline and background.

I continued to draw as I listened to help me understand the story. After the first line, I drew parts of the story and then continued to add in-depth to the drawing and make them more pronounced and varied in detail to show the change happening and the scenery. I finished listening to the recording and removed my headphones to see Mr. Cameron talking to a few other students who had completed the current task. While he is looking around to see when we would all finish like he told us he would at the start of the term. He stood up and walked over to me with a smile on his face. "Hey, Mark, how are you doing?"

I smiled before saying, "I'm doing good. How are you?"

Mr. Cameron replied, "I'm good. What did you draw today to remember the story like we talked about last week?" This was a strategy he recommended to me to help me remember what I read in class as I could more easily remember what I drew compared to what I read.

I turned my sketchbook around to show him the crude but complete drawing for the story. The lines were smooth and in proportion, but there could be more detail, and the sketch wasn't the most accurate.

It got the idea across, though, as Mr. Cameron said, "This looks amazing, Mark. How long did this take you?"

I shrugged as I didn't keep track of time when I was drawing, so I said. "I don't know, a few listen-throughs of the story."

"That is very impressive, Mark." Mr. Cameron saw that everyone looked to be done with the assignment and stood up from his kneeling position. "I'll talk to you later, Mark. Right now, I need to do the next part of today's lesson." Moving over to the center of the room, Mr. Cameron had a smile on his face as he said, "So, what do you people think the purpose of you reading that?"

Scott, the student next to me, raised his hand with a smile. He was different from the rest of the class as he was supposed to be one of the peer helpers to set an example for others. He said, "Weren't we supposed to learn about the new assignment and ways to do it?"

Mr. Cameron nodded to Scott and spoke, "Yes, that was part of the purpose, but what unit did the story you just read connect to?"

Scott appeared to be thinking before answering. "I don't know, abandonment?"

Mr. Cameron nodded. "That is one of the themes, but what about the type of writing, class?"

This time, Jasmine raised her hand, and Mr. Cameron called on her. "Does this relate to flash fiction?"

"Yes, it does. That is the style of writing or genre. There are many types of writing out there to be explored and used. The problem is learning how to make and use them. So that is the subject of this unit and the final project for the semester. You will need to choose a genre, or otherwise known as a writing style, to make one of the topics covered in this unit. You will need to develop a project and tell me the idea either verbally, through text, sign, or any other means of communication you want to use so I can understand what you plan to do. Now, what did you all think of the text, and you can explain what you understand through any medium you can do in under three minutes. I will give you prep time for this class, but I would like everyone to have gone by the end of the middle of the next class. Now, if anyone is ready to give an explanation, you may raise your hand."

My hand out of our small group moved up after a few seconds, and Mr. Cameron called me up to the front to talk about what I understood. I grabbed my sketchbook and showed the page I had drawn to the class with a smile. The group was small, so I felt comfortable talking to this group about what I had drawn.

The sketch showed the young child getting out of his pod with the person claiming to be his brother standing by. In the background, I had an image of the hangar door framing the image opening in the background. On the young child's head was a contraption removed from his head by the other person in the room. The drawing was just a sketch at this point, but it could be turned into a wonderful drawing if I ever finished coloring in the sketch.

"So, Mark, what did you understand from the reading? I see you did a very in-depth drawing, but I am wondering what you learned from the reading."

"I learned about accepting support to leave behind your old life for a better, new one." I swallowed, hoping my answer worked for what Mr. Cameron was looking for. Mr. Cameron looked around our small group with a smile to see if anyone would respond.

"Nice job, Mark. Now, what did the rest of the class understand from what Mark showed?" Scott raised a hand up to answer the question. "Yes, Scott," Mr. Cameron said.

Scott replied, "I think that Mark was showing the understanding of the motivations of the younger character in his drawing and explanation."

Mr. Cameron, with a clap, said, "Okay, any other questions or comments before he goes to sit down?"

Jasmine raised her hand, and Mr. Cameron called on Jasmine, and she said, "Mark, what did you think about the youngest child leaving the only home that they had known?"

I remained silent for a bit before saying, "That is hard to answer, but I think that it was a development for the character to grow." The whole class nodded to my response. When no one else raised a hand, I went to sit down with my sketchbook.

Mr. Cameron then said, "Is anyone else ready to come up and explain what they learned? If not, we can have work time until the end of class and do the next class if that works for everyone. Remember that it would be next Thursday, so you would need to remember this over the day off. Is that okay with you all?" The rest of the group nodded and got to work on doing what they planned on presenting to the class.

Mr. Cameron walked over to me with a smile on his face and said, "Hey, Mark, great job with that piece of artwork. I enjoyed how you demonstrated the story. Keep up the great work and let me know if you ever need help understanding the story—good job showing and volunteering today. I liked how you stood up and were the first one to go. If you ever need any help or want helpful feedback on the work you are doing, let me know."

"Okay." Mr. Cameron walked away, and he began to wander the classroom. This was, as he said, to make sure everyone was getting the help they needed to succeed.

I started to finish the sketch for Steve. I finished the forms and got ready to ink them in after I got approval. I had made very light marks that would be easy to erase and left little marks on the paper when I inked in the image. I pulled out the graphic novel sketch and finished the ending characters and characters that I hadn't drawn yet. Finishing the wolf's various parts and angled images took me most of the rest of the class, but I finished that part. Pulling out the scenes I had already drawn, I got ready to add detail to the un-inked portions when the lights began to dim and brighten to signal the end of the day.

Chapter Nineteen
PACKING FOR HOME

PUTTING MY GRAPHIC NOVEL sketchbook into my bag, I got ready to head out after sending a quick text to Steve to see if we could meet up before we would head home. I wanted to get the approval of the sketch for his commission. Steve texted back, asking for me to meet him up by the front of the school.

I headed out into the small river of students flowing out of the school and into cars, bikes, or just walking. I reached the school's front and saw Steve standing near the parking area's edge, looking around.

Walking up to him, I tapped him on the shoulder from behind and said, "How are you doing?"

Steve turned around and responded that he was doing good and was ready to see the sketch. I opened my backpack and showed the sketch to Steve to get approval. The sketch wasn't of the best quality, but it worked for an example and to get approval for inking in and adding detail.

Steve looked at the drawing for a few seconds before he said, "That looks amazing, Mark. I'm excited to see what else you do with it."

I looked at Steve and said, "Thanks. I'm glad you like it."

"It is amazing, Mark. That would take me ages to even get that half as good, and you did it so quickly."

"Thank you?" I wasn't sure how to reply. I hadn't really been complimented on sketches like this as I rarely showed anyone them. I would show them the image later, but I wanted to see what Steve thought of this and if he might want any changes.

"No problem. Thank you for doing this for me. I'm very much like how this is turning out." Steve gave me a large smile when he said that. "I need to head out now. I'll talk with you later. I hope you have a good day."

I walked out and down the sidewalk to Josh's car, the sun shining down onto me, being barely blocked by the shade of the surrounding trees.

"Hey, Mark, ready to go and pack?" I remained quiet, heading to the car, climbing in, and curling up as much as possible. The day had been stressful, and I didn't want to go back to my old home. "I know; I'm sorry, Mark, you can stay in the car if you want, but I don't have time to take you back to the apartment before my next appointment."

Holding up a hand from my curled-up position, I signed *OK*. I knew that I would need to do this, but I didn't want to. I needed to face my parents eventually, and I couldn't keep running away. I had a place that was safe, and if I needed to go, so I should be able to talk to them without fear, but it was still full of fear of what might happen. I know Josh now cared for me, but I didn't know if he would be willing to fight our parents for me.

I think he yelled at our parents last time I was home, but I don't know what the conversation was about. The car lurched forward, and we began to drive away from the school. The car shook as it got up to speed, but we smoothed out over time. I closed my eyes, trying to block out the sunlight streaming through the window. We pulled to a stop across from the house, and I could see both cars in the driveway. I got up, put in my earplugs, and slid on my sunglasses. I no longer cared what would happen as I would just say I had a migraine which was the truth partially. I was nearing sensory overload, and I knew that I would need to run straight to my room to calm down again.

Leaving the car, I dragged my feet under me, and with Josh moving at the same speed at me looking over to him, I saw what I was told was worried on his face.

Looking over, I said, "I'm fine, Josh. I just have a headache."

"Remember, Mark, if you need anything, let me know, and I'll try to help." Josh's voice quivered as he spoke.

We walked forward and reached the doorway that was closed. Josh tried the handle, and the door was locked. Josh pulled out a set of keys from his pocket to unlock the door. The key slid in and turned until a loud click came from the door, meaning it was unlocked. Josh moved his hand down to the easy-grip ledge handle and swung the door open.

Walking into the quiet house, I began to hear a stove going. Moving up the stairs, I reached my room and entered. Seeing an almost bare room, I began to continue packing up. I left my desk empty and only a few books left on the shelves to be put into boxes later.

Josh joined me in my room and saw me packing; he began to help. After letting me in, I moved games up off the shelves and into the boxes Josh grabbed from the car. I don't know where the boxes came from, only that we could use them. The packing took a few hours until the bottom door opened, and someone came inside.

They said, "I am back, Heather. Is someone here? The front door was unlocked?" After that, it went quiet. My dad had come home from something, and that scared me. Normally, he would be at work or home right now. That was unless he was meeting with someone about changing what was happening to the city and becoming more friendly to people with visible disabilities.

Continuing to pack, I blocked out my thoughts and just continued to pack. My vision was getting fuzzy, but I continued to pack into the boxes and bags, ready to leave when Josh said we were done.

I finished the shelf I had been doing before I could stop and curled up on my mostly bare bed. Only a few stuffed animals and blankets remained from my previous nest of comfort. I had made it on the bed; curling up, I sat and waited to hear what Josh would say; not wanting to see the world, I closed my eyes and buried myself into the few blankets I had left on the bed.

Josh's voice said quietly to me, "Hey, Mark. Are you doing okay?"

I remained quiet on the bed, curled up, waiting to feel better. The lights dimmed, and I heard that Josh continued to pack, occasionally stopping for a bit, asking if I was okay before continuing.

"The room is packed, Mark. We need to come back later, but we should go home now with a few boxes." I sat up and looked around at the packed room. All that was left unpacked were staying here like the bed, shelves, desk, and dresser. Getting up to my feet, landing on the ground, softly giving me a slight jolt into awareness from my sleepy state, I moved over and grabbed the box that was labeled fabric and sewing machine. I left the room quietly, carrying the heavy box. My feet made some sound on the wooden floor, causing a few jolts to go through me. Reaching the stairway, I head downstairs and see my parents sitting in the living room, looking at each other and talking quietly.

Chapter Twenty
FAMILIES TALK

"Hello, Mark, Josh; how are you two doing?" My dad said this when he saw me reach the bottom of the stairs, Josh following me. He was looking at me like I was a curiosity at a museum.

Looking over, I saw what I was told was worried on his face, and my mom began to talk. "So, I see you are continuing to move out, Mark." Her face was stretched out as she spoke, her eyes tight.

I nodded my head, not wanting to talk.

My mom's head was down until she looked up at the space behind me, and something caused her to react, and she said quickly, "Okay, do you want to stay for dinner?" I knew Josh was behind me, but I don't know what he would have done to change her behavior and invite me to dinner.

I tilted my head at that, and she continued to talk, "I made lasagna and cheesy garlic bread for dinner tonight. If I remember correctly, you used to love this meal when you were younger." Mom was correct, but I now preferred burgers and curry even though I still had a soft spot for that type of food. She made that last for me when I was ten before I got diagnosed, but she still had it on the menu. I used to manage by just not being home. I would stay over with a friend, so I could stay strong and not break down.

Josh, from behind me, said, "Mark, I think it should be okay for us to have dinner here if you want. I know you used to like that type of food. George and I don't really have the time to make that food unless you want it to be frozen."

I decided to speak in front of my parents again, which I hadn't done recently. "We can stay for dinner, I guess." My voice was shaky as I felt that we would be having a conversation I had been holding off for the past few years. I knew that this needed to happen, but I was not sure what to say. "First, we should put the boxes in the car." My voice was stronger at that time, as I wanted to be able to leave quickly if I needed to.

My mom said, "How about you go and help them put the boxes in the car, Brent?" My dad got up from where he was sitting next to my mom. He moved over to us before Josh and I headed out to the car to place the boxes and bags inside. We walked in and out with my dad helping with a few of the loads until the car was stuffed full of boxes and bags to the point where only three seats remained empty, one for George and me and then the driver's seat. This was because we needed to go grocery shopping later and possibly not have time to empty the car, depending on when dinner ended.

Heading back inside, we headed to the table, which I had barely sat at in recent times, normally eating in my room, or at a friend's place, instead of here at my parent's house. Sitting down in my old chair, which I used on Friday to eat breakfast, I preferred to eat in the same spot every day, at least when I was using the table. If you looked at the feet and bar of the chair, there was wear and tear underneath from all the bouncing and kicking I had done. My family didn't really understand, but if they didn't see it, they had an off-sight out-of-mind point of view for my fidgeting.

Dad said, "So, Mark, how are you doing in school?" Why do they care now when I have asked for help in the past? You gave it but didn't care to change explanations so I could understand.

Responding back with, "I am doing okay; in art doing well right now."

My dad's face scrunched, but he gave a small, twisted smile after Josh gave a slight growl. "That's great, Mark." He replied with. "How are your other classes?"

"They are okay. My English teacher enjoys my artwork summaries." I'm not sure if my parents know what I am talking about.

Before either of my parents responded, Josh jumped in, saying. "Could you explain what those are, Mark? I am curious as I learned of something similar, possibly in my college writing course."

I smiled at Josh; he acted as the peacekeeper between us; that must be a hard task. I responded with, "I draw to help me remember what we read and what the teacher says in class as writing down notes doesn't really work for me."

"That's nice," my mom said as she gave me a smile.

Mom continued by saying, "So what have you been doing in your classes? I heard they have changed a lot since Josh was in high school."

"They have changed every class to have an interpreter for the students who use sign language." That was one massive change that I remembered being different from when Josh went to high school. I was surprised she asked as she should know due to how much she campaigned against the changes. I answered in a monotone voice that was normal for me, "Also, I have been doing good in my classes, and my accommodations are helping me." I wondered how my parents would react to learning I used my accommodations.

Chapter Twenty-One
UNEXPECTED SOURCE OF SUPPORT

LOOKING OVER, I SAW my dad starting to have a frown on his face at me while my mom still had a smile on her face. The table began to feel like it was shrinking due to how my dad was looking at me. As he looked at me, a timer went off, and my mom stood up from the table saying, "Dinners ready, I'll go bring it to the table. If you want to help, bring over the food, Brent. That would be appreciated." My dad got up and walked away into the kitchen to grab the food. A pleasant smell of tomato, cooked cheese, and meat filled the air. In the air, I smelled garlic and onion along with spices that I couldn't place.

Looking over to Josh, I saw a neutral face, neither smiling nor frowning. I waved over to him, hoping he would wave back at me so I might smile at him and lift his spirits. I continued to wave, but Josh didn't look my way. I stopped waving when I heard my dad say, "Mark, what are you doing waving like that?" I shrunk back into my chair, and that snapped Josh from what seemed to be a trance.

"Dad, Mark is fine in what he is doing. You don't need to ask when you already know the answer," Josh's voice had changed. His voice was deeper, and he held a growl.

"Yes, but he needs to learn not to do that all the time." Dad's face appeared like he normally did when I did anything; he didn't consider it normal in his mind.

"Honey, remember what we talked about," my mom said with a weird look on her face.

"Yes, I remember, dear, but Mark should still not act that way." My dad's face was stern as he spoke.

"Brent, let's put the food down and have dinner." My mom's voice sounded harsh, and she placed the dish with the lasagna down, not so gently as the table rattled slightly. My dad sat down and stopped talking. My mom looked around as if she dared us to say anything against what she wanted. "So, Mark, anything interesting happened recently?"

"Yes." I just responded as many interesting things had happened, and I didn't know which one I was supposed to talk about.

"What happened, Mark?" My mom was looking at me, waiting for me to respond.

I shrunk back in my chair slightly, not wanting to talk. Looking around, I saw Josh giving me a smile, and my dad was looking away.

"Um, I guess, I um, I don't know, I moved, but you already knew that." Dad scoffed at that, but mom continued to smile at Josh and me. Josh nodded his head encouragingly. "I went to the local church for the art sale they had for people to sell what they have made or no longer need."

"What did you do there, Mark? Did you find a job to earn money?" Mom stared at me with a neutral face, and dad's face was scowling at me like he didn't want to hear this.

"I kind of found a job. I work selling my art at different fairs."

My dad then began to talk quickly, "I thought you knew you would never make a living with your art. I knew we should have discouraged you from doing such activities sooner. What are . . ."

Josh interrupted his sentence, "Dad. Mark's artwork is great, and he is selling it to people who enjoy what he makes."

"Do you think that matters, Josh? Do you honestly think that Mark will be able to make a living by just selling artwork?" Dad was harsh with his words. I had heard them before; that was why I had hidden this part of my life from them.

"Now, Brent, I think that if Josh supports Mark in this profession, Mark might be able to survive while doing that type of job." Mom was a calm voice of reason cutting through the arguing quickly.

"Yes, but Heather, think about it. How will Mark be able to support a family if he works like that?" Dad was kind of right though wrong at the same time, as I didn't want to be the only one supporting my family. I could support myself but not necessarily a partner or children. I wanted to be happy and working with my future partner and me would help with that.

"Dad, that doesn't matter. Mark is happy, and I will support him, and so should you. He is happy with such work, and he has people who support him and offer help and critique on the work." Josh was making me happy with my choice. He was right. I had people who enjoyed and supported my work happily, and that is all that matters. I knew what I wanted to do, so I will continue to do my artwork and make people happy with what I make.

Mom spoke up and calmly said, "I agree with Josh, Honey. We didn't support Mark when he started, but we can fix that mistake now. We can support him in his work. So please let us do this for him; let us help him with his passion." Why is mom saying that when she had such a different response when I was younger and first brought this up?

"Fine, if that is what you want, I will eat later." Dad then walked off into the distance, and I could faintly hear thudding up the stairs.

"Sorry about that, Mark. I know that I may not have been the best in the past, but I want to do better now. Seeing all the other families, I realized that we were no longer the same. You are barely home. You spend most of your time away from home now. I worked hard to be a good mother, but I feel that I have failed at that. So please let me try and do better from now on. I want to help you, but I don't know how to right now. I will still try to help and do better as I want us to be a family again. I am hoping you will be willing to move back in soon after we get a better relationship." Mom's face had a smile as she spoke, her eyes open, looking at me. A few tears left her eyes as she was giving the talk. Though she was trying to look me in the eye, I just continued to move my head away from her eyes. "Mark, could I look in your eyes? I want for you to know I am telling the truth."

Quickly, I yelled out, "I believe you. I don't like looking at others in the eyes." I became quiet after that, just looking around the room, waiting for a response.

My mom sighed before saying, "Alright then, Mark. Thank you for believing me. I am sorry I wasn't there for you when you were younger, offering more support, but I want to help you now."

"Okay, mom," I said quietly as my head was beginning to hurt as I was speaking.

Josh moved, leaned forward, and had begun to open his mouth, but my mom spoke first. "I am happy you understand. Let me know if there is anything I can do to help, Mark."

I just nodded my head. Then Josh began to talk in a quiet calm voice. "I think that we should eat, and then we should head out so Mark can go to sleep for school tomorrow."

"That sounds fair, Josh; let's eat, and then you two can head out. I hope you come again soon." My mom passed out the food to us, and we began to eat.

I hadn't had this food in a while. I covered my face in sauce and cheese. I could feel it covering my face, and I didn't want to have the sauce on my face, so I pulled out a napkin and I wiped my face. I smiled, happy to be eating one of my old comfort foods.

"So, are you enjoying the food, Mark?" Josh asked me after he finished eating. I still had part of my plate left to eat, but I was smiling, and my headache had lessened slightly.

"Yes, I am. How about you, do you like the food?" I had turned to Josh to ask the question just like I was told to.

"Yes, I do. Thank you for making this for us, Mom."

Mom had a smile on her face as we both said that we liked the food.

"See you later, Mom; Mark and I should get going soon." Josh had stood up, and I quickly joined him, wanting to leave the weird world I had found myself in.

Walking out of the room, Josh and I left for the car leaving behind my mom in the dining room. As we left the house, I turned around and saw my mom smiling, looking out over us with crinkles around her eyes.

Chapter Twenty-Two
RELAX WITH HELP

THE RIDE BACK TO the apartment was peaceful and calm. We took back roads to avoid traffic on the way to the apartment, which was downtown. We barely talked as we drove to the apartment; Josh had a smile on his face, though, as he drove through the streets.

Parking in front of the apartment building, Josh turned to me and spoke. "Hey, Mark, you make pride flag weavings, correct?"

"Yes, how come?" I was curious as I didn't know why Josh would want one of those, maybe for a friend. I know I made them on request for Valentine and a few of my other friends like Kyle. I also made them for myself as I was currently questioning my own attractions and gender. I had been asking Valentine questions recently. I had been thinking about who I liked and who I knew to talk to about this. I didn't want to talk to my parents or Josh about it yet, but I hoped I would become more comfortable around Josh to talk to him about this eventually. I knew my family accepted a few of their friends who were gay, but I didn't know about them in the family.

Josh looked around before he turned to me and spoke. "Just wondering, we could possibly put a few up around the apartment."

"If you want to, I can make them for you, but I would need to charge a commission to be fair to all of my friends." I hoped Josh would be okay with that request.

Josh replied by saying, "That's fine, Mark. I am willing to pay commission."

"Depends on the size and amount being ordered and if they are woven or sewn." Normally, I made the sewn ones cheaper as they were easier to make. Still, they could also be more expensive depending on the fabric and size due to the material.

"Okay, I'll need to talk to George about that, but I don't think he will mind. Now how about we head inside, and we can talk to him then." Josh opened his car door into the now-empty road and moved to the sidewalk quickly. I followed, and we entered the apartment. Unlocking the apartment, the door opened, and I could faintly smell popcorn in the air.

I heard him yell out to the apartment from Josh, "George, we are back."

George popped out from the hallway and gave us a smile. He then asked, "Hey, how was your visit back with your parents?"

"It was okay. We had dinner there like I told you." When had Josh told George that we were having dinner with our parents? I thought we hadn't planned for dinner, but maybe they had, and mom assumed I still like the same food. I don't know, but I will give the benefit of the doubt to Josh.

"Okay, do you need help unpacking the car?" George had stood up from the couch and moved over to stand in front of Josh and me.

"Sure, Mark, how about you go to your room and unpack the boxes George and I bring up?" Josh had turned to me when he said that. Nodding my head, I moved over to my room. Opening the door, I sat on my bed and waited.

I heard the door open and close. I sat and waited, lost in thought, thinking about how my mom had changed her actions to me. She had started to support me in my art, apparently. Why did she change so much? I didn't know what had happened or how to react to the change. I didn't want to make the wrong assumption about what will happen with my mom in the future. I felt alone right now, and I was, but I didn't want to be alone. I started to cry as I thought about what was happening. My life was changing too quickly for me to keep up with what was happening. I stood up and began to walk back and forth before crashing back on my bed face-down.

I didn't want to think. I just wanted to have my nest again. I wanted to be able to curl up and block out the world. I wanted to have Josh and Steve next to me to help me feel better. I wanted to talk to Jaden, but I would need to wait until tomorrow. I didn't know what to do. I laid in my bed alone until I heard the door open with a small creak.

Josh and George entered my room, carrying boxes. I sat up, cheeks red and eyes puffy, at least according to the mirror in the room.

Josh stood in front of me and said, "Hey, Mark, are you doing okay? Anything I can do to help?"

Nodding my head, I stood up and signed, asking for a *hug*. I wanted comfort and to know that someone was around me. Josh opened his arms to me, and I walked forward into his embrace. Wrapping my arms around his body, I relaxed into his grasp. I felt better and moved my arms, and Josh released me.

I stood back up and began to unpack a few boxes into the room, throwing my blankets and pillows onto the bed haphazardly.

"Mark, would you like me or George to stay in the room with you while you unpack?" Nodding my head at them, I smiled and continued to unpack. "Are you okay if we switch off, so we don't get tired?" Nodding my head at them, I continue to try and remake my nest of blankets. "Okay, George, how about you go grab some boxes, and I'll go next."

"Okay, just make sure your brother is okay, Josh." George then left the room, heading back down to the car based on what was said.

The room was beginning to fill with my stuff. George would ask me where to put different items. I would attempt to gesture, assuming he didn't know sign until he began to sign at me, asking if I wanted to use sign language instead of gesturing. I would point and sign where to put different items in the room, such as to put certain books on different shelves so they were in an organized mess where I could find them. I would tell George and my brother to put games on the bottom shelf in a tower.

After a few minutes, I felt better, and it was getting easier to speak again though I remained quiet, waiting to figure out what to say. I continued to unpack into my room, which was beginning to get full. Finally, the last box got brought in by George. While George had been grabbing the boxes, Josh had been looking at me while unpacking. I think he might have been trying to figure out what I was thinking. The ground was comfortable for me to sit on. The ground meant comfort because it was always around me; it was a constant in my life. Whenever I would enter sensory overload, I would lay on the floor or a large flat surface like a bed. Floor meant that I wouldn't fall over as easily as if I was in a chair. So, I wouldn't get hurt by falling, and others were more likely to see that I needed help.

I sat and continued to unpack, waiting to hear what Josh or George would say. Finally, all the boxes got unpacked, and I jumped onto my bed and curled up under my pile of blankets. The weight was pressing down on me from all the quilts. My weighted blanket was next to me, and I tried to pull it over me to be under the pile of blankets.

I looked up from my bed and saw Josh and George smiling at me. I was curled up on my bed, smiling from the sensation of the weighted blanket and all the textures surrounding me. Josh then began to speak, saying, "Hey Mark, George and I have something to tell you. Do you want us to tell you here or out in the dining room? Either is fine, but I want to give you a choice."

Deciding to climb out of my bed, I signed the *dining room*, walked out to the room, and waited for them to join me. Entering the room, they looked what I was told meant nervous.

Josh said, "So, I don't know how to tell you this in an easy way, but I will try to do it quickly." I nodded my head, looking at Josh and George with hands interlocked. He paused for a moment and said, "George and I are engaged."

I just nodded, looking at them before smiling. I know now that I had another resource in my family to talk to about this stuff. I already had been reading online for help and to figure stuff out and asking questions of Valentine. I felt that I could possibly tell Josh about my own feelings at some point, as we were growing close, and he had trusted me. I said, "Okay, Josh." I walked forward with my arms open to give a hug. All three of us held each other in a hug for a few minutes. It felt like I had lost a burden and was now free to explore.

We then let go, and George began to speak, "Thank you for accepting Josh and me. I know I haven't known you long, but the amount of time I have spent talking to your brother about you, I feel like I know you." George had a smile on his face as he spoke to me. His face then changed as he looked at Josh and me. "Josh, you might want to tell Mark what happened recently."

"Yes, I should, but tonight should be a night to celebrate, so let's celebrate, and we can talk tomorrow. Tomorrow, you don't have school because it is a teacher's workday if I remember correctly. So how about we go out and celebrate for lunch tomorrow?"

"So, what do you think of George and me being engaged? I know we waited a bit to tell you, but we wanted to give you a day where nothing happens to process. You're moving also impacted as it meant we might need to hide around you, and we didn't want that to happen. If you have any questions, just ask us. We have been dating for a few years and got engaged this year. I'm sorry for not telling you I was gay earlier." Josh looked at me with what I think was either a worry or nervousness tone in his voice, head tilted down.

I said, "It works, whatever makes you happy." I honestly didn't care if Josh continued to support me and be kind. I could care less who Josh was in love with. I was just happy to have my brother back, and I didn't want anything to ruin that. I might even talk to them about how they feel and how they learned that they were gay. I had talked with Valentine and Kyle about this, but I was still confused and wanted to learn more. I wanted to be able to figure out who I was. Valentine thinks that I might be asexual, which could fit, but I'm not sure. I still need to explore and experiment before I learn who I am. I feel that I'm not straight, but I'm not sure what else I am.

"Thank you. How about we head to bed, and in the morning, we can talk some more as I am starting to get tired." I nodded my head to Josh, and we went to our bedrooms, me to mine and Josh and George to theirs.

Chapter Twenty-Three

ALLIES INFORMING BREAKFAST

JOSH AND GEORGE HAD told me last night that they were engaged. I was happy for them, but I wasn't sure what else I felt about that. I wanted them to be happy, and I knew they were good for each other, but I just didn't know. I thought it was good that I didn't have school today so I could spend the day processing. I needed to think about this and get ready to face the challenges that would be happening today.

I curled into my blankets and got ready to leave my cocoon of blankets and greet the world. I got up and smiled, remembering that I wasn't in my parent's house and was with Josh. The wooden floor felt cold, so I went to put on some socks. I grabbed a pair of nice thick fluffy ones that would keep my feet warm. Putting them on under my fleece pajamas, I got ready to head out and greet Josh and George.

I could smell meat being cooked and hear a few sizzling items being cooked on the stove. Walking in, I saw both Josh and George moving around the kitchen cooking. George was at the stove, and Josh was prepping items to be added to the pan.

Josh then turned around after putting a knife down and started to say, "Hey, how are you doing this morning?"

"I'm doing good, tired, but good." I smiled at them and saw eggs and bacon were cooking along with something in the oven. I would guess sausages or muffins, possibly both, but I couldn't tell.

Josh smiled at me before going back to prepping food after saying, "That's good to hear. So today, George and I would like to tell you a few things that will be happening soon."

I just nodded my head before saying, "Okay," before moving over to the table to sit down and wait for the food to finish. After a few minutes, the food was finished, and a plate was put in front of me containing an egg, a muffin, and two sausages. After letting the food cool, I began to eat.

Josh said, "Our aunt and uncle are coming over to visit. I stayed with them for the past few years on weekends when I was off to college. They are not like our parents and are supportive and accepting of almost everyone." I just nodded my head, barely remembering them as I hadn't seen them since the city had started to change. I hope they would accept the news that was accommodating for people with various needs. "Also, since you know that George and I are engaged, we are getting married next year during the summer. We have told my parents that we were dating but not that we were engaged yet. George's parents know that we are engaged, but we still have yet to tell our parents the full story, Mark." I was getting worried about not knowing what would happen soon with this. Did my parents accept this couple, or did they refuse them? "Don't worry, Mark, our parents are fine with it, just shocked. They weren't expecting it, but they aren't spouting hate for me being gay, so that is a plus. That is another reason they let you move in with me because our parents thought that the two of us could offer more support than just me. How do I put this? George has a few siblings with autism, and our parents thought that that knowledge could help you adjust. So, Mark, are you okay with keeping the secret of our engagement from our parents?"

"Sure, Josh." I finished eating before getting up and heading into my room. I pulled out my drawing material and tried to figure out what to draw. Normally, it would be easy for me to figure out what to draw, but now it was difficult. I didn't know what to draw due to so many new things happening. Holding out my sketch pad, I decided to just let my brain wander and draw simultaneously. This piece would most likely be terrible or good, depending on my mind and how my muscle memory worked for me today.

I chose a light gray pencil that would erase easily and began to let my mind wander as I drew. Not knowing what to think about, only knowing that I needed to process what had been happening, and drawing was one of my ways of processing.

I was thinking about my family and how my aunt and uncle visiting could change what had happened. From a few of their rants, I could remember they supported people who were not standard. My brother just reinforced that idea. The support they offered to others in their area was great as they tried to help people of all types. One of the few memories is my aunt talking to my mom about me needing to be diagnosed. My uncle, however, talked to my dad about my brother and how he should also get tested based on the stories my parents told them when we were younger. My uncle claimed that Josh was masking to fit in, but my dad and mom refused to believe that.

I continued to draw, lost in thought. What should I say to my aunt and uncle when I haven't seen them in a few years? I hadn't even called them on the phone recently. I knew that Josh had spoken to them recently as he said that sometimes, he drives over to their house on occasion to spend the weekend when he needs a break from school.

My aunt and mom were strong-willed and didn't like to change their opinion though my aunt was open to more changes than my mom. What my aunt and uncle's work did to change their community was staggering if the news was to be believed. They had changed the school to have more sensory-friendly lights and more ramps next to the stairs. The schools in the area they lived in were catching up to the schools in my city if not moving faster.

Stopping in my thought process, I felt my pencil slide off the page, so I decided to look closely at what I had drawn. It was a few small sketches combined into one circle. It was reminiscent of the collage I had made of Josh and me, just on a smaller scale. The shading in a few places was harsh, so I should smooth that out. This was different; it was an image of multi-events showing schools, people, and parks. In total, I think around seven images were highlighting what my aunt and uncle had done from what I had learned in school, from my mom and dad, along with the news. This piece was done in a spiral, starting at the center and going out in chronological order.

It took up about half of my sketchbook page, which was around six inches by six inches. Some of the images were in the style of my graphic novel, and drawing styles got mixed in. This was most likely because it was muscle memory and that I wasn't looking at the page the whole time using memory to draw.

I had finished this drawing for the moment to the best of my ability. I had worked hard just drawing this small piece, and luckily, my muscle memory from all the drawing I had done kicked in.

Now it was time to draw a different piece to help me process what had been happening with Josh. I flipped to another page and began to draw again. I let my mind begin to wander around again just to think. I knew that I would need to speak to Jaden soon, but drawing was at least helping me not to be as frantic as I could be.

I didn't know what I should do now. I lay in bed, thinking about what happened last time. I wanted to be accepted and cared for by my family. I cared for Josh, so I would accept and support him in what might happen with our relationship with our parents. I knew that I wanted to help Josh, and hopefully, help would help me. Josh came out to me, and I was still figuring out what I identified as right now; I wasn't sure. The stories that Valentine told me when they were learning about their identity resonated with me, and I felt like I was going through the same thing.

I wanted to be accepted for who I am fully, even if that changes in the future, and I think that Josh and George might help me to be able to accept who I am. They will help me work through who I am if I ask, but first, I want to talk to some of my friends and find out how I can support them before asking them to support me.

I laid in my cocoon of blankets, trying to fall asleep as I thought about what was happening in my life and all the changes that were happening. Tomorrow would be a new day, and I would be working toward a brighter life now that I can see more of who I am instead of just feeling like a blank slate filled with white and black pain. Now color was falling and changing me.

Glossary

Accommodations: differing ways to help people to succeed and be on a fair playing level as people without a mental or physical disability.

ADHD: Attention deficit hyperactivity disorder.

Advocate: a person who offers help and tries to get people needed help or accommodations. This includes trying to get varying rights for people depending on race, sexual orientation, physical and mental ability, age, gender, and so forth.

Autism: a condition where people have trouble communicating and understanding others' feelings. This makes it harder for them to communicate wants to others or different needs.

Chewies: items designed to be safe for people to chew on to gain oral stimulation.

Crisis counseling: a person may need the immediate help of a mental health professional due to having some type of crisis. Such a crisis can be caused by past trauma, after or during a panic attack, when a person is having trouble with their physical wellbeing, and more. This is when you seek the help of a counselor either in person or through a helpline, depending.

Dyslexia: a disorder that makes it harder to read different languages due to mixing up letters or order of words.

Fidgets: toys designed to be used for stimulation and to help with stimming. Examples are fidget spinners and cubes. They give input to the body in a controlled manner.

Nonverbal: unable to communicate in a verbal manner due to either a mental or physical reason.

Occupational therapy: therapy designed to help with fine motor movements like writing and other skills used in day-to-day life. Mostly focuses on repetitive motions to help build up strength and muscle memory.

Panic attack: suddenly experiencing panic or fear caused by a perceived threat. This can cause a physical reaction that is either minor or intense, depending on the person and the situation.

Sensory overload: a response to a situation that is either over simulating or expected to be over-stimulating could have fear or anger involved or a complete shutdown of the mind to blank out and restart. The first part with anger or fear is also known as a meltdown. The part about shutting down the mind is also known as a shutdown.

Stimming: behavior to provide stimulus to the body and mind. May form in repeated phrases and actions such as moving hands in a certain way.

Speech therapy: a place where students are taught how to speak correctly and different means of communication if they are unable to speak. One method of non-verbal communication is a communication binder or using sign language.

Gay: a term that can refer to the Queer/LGBTQIA+ community at large. It can also refer to individuals who are attracted to the same gender presentation of them.

GSA/QSA: gender and sexuality alliance or gay-straight alliance/ Queer, straight alliance. This is a club or group normally in a school that focuses on providing a safe and accepting space for members of the Queer/ LGBTQIA+ community to gather and talk. It can also be used as a learning space for allies of the community and people who are just now learning about their identity.

Nonbinary: under the trans umbrella, a person who identifies as anything other than strictly man or strictly women.

Trans: any person whose gender identity differs from their sex assigned at birth.

Mx.: pronounced mix is an honorific that some people choose to use to refer to themselves and is gender-neutral.

CPSIA information can be obtained
at www.ICGtesting.com
Printed in the USA
LVHW090919030322
712197LV00011B/59